"Jane!"

As *Raku Nau* got closer to the finish, the stakes seemed to be going up, and the competition was rising. Nobody was safe now.

Vanessa boosted Buzz into the tree and then pulled herself up. Maybe the tree would hold them, maybe it wouldn't. There was only one way to find out. And taking risks was turning into second nature here on Shadow Island.

No winning without boldness, Vanessa thought. She couldn't remember who had told her that. But she remembered something else—something that her social studies teacher had said one day. *The adventure you get is the one that you're ready for*. So maybe they were ready for this, right now.

And ready or not, here they came.

STRANDED
SHADOW ISLAND
BOOK 2: THE SABOTAGE

JEFF PROBST
and CHRIS TEBBETTS

PUFFIN BOOKS
An Imprint of Penguin Group (USA)

PUFFIN BOOKS
Published by the Penguin Group
Penguin Group (USA) LLC
345 Hudson Street
New York, New York 10014

USA / Canada / UK / Ireland / Australia / New Zealand / India / South Africa / China
penguin.com
A Penguin Random House Company

First published in the United States of America by Puffin Books,
an imprint of Penguin Young Readers Group, 2015

CIP Data is available

Puffin Books ISBN: 978-0-14-751389-2

Printed in the United States of America

1 3 5 7 9 10 8 6 4 2

To CJ,

Thank you for the inspiration.

Your texts and funny photos always made me laugh.

Your spirit is alive in these pages, and your torch

will always shine bright.

—JP

THE SABOTAGE

CHAPTER 1

Buzz stumbled along in a daze—sleepless, hungry, thirsty, and scared.

But angry, too.

As angry as he'd ever been. The vine around his wrists burned a groove into the skin, a little deeper every time he tried to wriggle free of its knots. And the pain made him only madder.

"Why are we going this way?" he asked, but it was a waste of breath, and he knew it. His captor, Chizo, didn't speak English any more than Buzz spoke the Nukula language of this island. The only response that came back was a yank on the vine, as Chizo pulled him along like some kind of animal on a leash.

Buzz wracked his brain, replaying the last hour over and over. It was hard to imagine how this could have been avoided. The capture itself had happened in the dark, without warning. One moment, he'd been staring at the campfire, taking the last watch of the night. The next moment, two strong hands had closed around him. One palm had covered his mouth while the other snaked around his chest, squeezing the air out of his lungs as he'd been dragged right off the log where he'd been sitting. There had been no chance to get away, or even call out for help. Chizo had pulled him out of camp as smoothly and silently as a move in a game of Jenga.

Except, of course, this was no game. It was *Raku Nau*.

They were headed in exactly the wrong direction. The whole point of *Raku Nau* was to be among the first sixteen competitors to cross Cloud Ridge, to the east. But as Buzz stumbled along through a long stretch of unfamiliar woods, the sun was just rising at his back. That meant they were headed west.

The longer it went on, the clearer it had become that

this competition had no rules. Capture and sabotage came with the territory. Buzz could see that now, but *now* was too late to do anything about it.

As for what Chizo had in mind—how he was going to pull off this sabotage and still keep himself in the competition—it was impossible to say. Meanwhile, every step they took was one step farther away from Cloud Ridge, farther from finishing *Raku Nau*, and, most important for Buzz, farther away from any chance of ever making it home again.

This wasn't over, he reminded himself. There was still the chance he could be rescued by the others. Or maybe he could figure out some way of escaping on his own.

That meant it wasn't hopeless. Not yet.

But it sure was getting close.

CHAPTER 2

Vanessa tried to breathe. Tried to focus. Tried not to freak out entirely.

It was hard enough, just working to survive in a place like this, and a competition like *Raku Nau*. But waking up to find her little brother kidnapped was making it nearly impossible to keep from falling into a full-scale panic.

"Which way do you think they went?" she yelled.

Nobody seemed to hear. It was chaos in the camp. Carter was in the woods, still shouting Buzz's name. Jane was running up and down the shore looking for any kind of telltale footprints. And Mima was already up to her knees in the water, motioning for everyone to get on the raft so they could go.

"We have to make sure he's not still here!" Jane called out, illustrating her words with hand motions so that Mima, their one Nukula ally, could understand.

"Mima's right! He's gone! Let's move!" Vanessa called back, as evenly as she could. Jane was the youngest, at nine years old, and far stronger than she looked. But she was still just a kid.

So was Buzz, for that matter. He and Carter were both eleven. No matter how long this nightmare went on, Vanessa was always going to feel responsible for the other three, even if she was just thirteen herself.

They never should have been here in the first place. It was like the opposite of winning Powerball—a zillion-to-one odds of bad luck that just went on and on. It felt like far more than two weeks ago that the four siblings had been shipwrecked on Nowhere Island. They'd struggled, but they'd managed to survive there, thirteen days alone in the middle of the South Pacific.

The cruelest twist of all was being swept from that

island to this one, literally within hours of being found. But nobody could have predicted the swift-moving tide that had carried them away from their parents, even while the newly reunited family had waited for a rescue chopper to take them back to the mainland.

Vanessa shook her head as if those painful thoughts could be erased with a simple shake. There was no use focusing on everything that had gone wrong, anyway. No more thinking about good and bad luck. The only useful questions now were: *Where's Buzz?* And, *What do we need to do to get him back?*

"Come on, Jane!" Carter shouted. "Vanessa's right. We need to move—right now!"

"We should have been gone five minutes ago," Vanessa said as they all waded into the water.

Mima seemed to agree. As they came closer, she hopped up onto the bamboo raft they would use to paddle across the bay and look for Buzz.

"Ekka-ka!" she said again, pointing east across the miles of water that lay ahead. It meant "this way" in

Nukula, and it was one of the few phrases Carter had managed to pick up in their few days here on the new island.

"Thank you," he told her in English.

Mima didn't have to wait for them like this, but she did it anyway. Carter only hoped that she was as glad for their help as he was for hers. She'd come into *Raku Nau* alone and had joined forces with them on the first day. The fact that she had no alliance within the Nukula tribe hinted at some larger story, but without any common language, it was hard to know what it might be.

Still, they never would have gotten this far without her, and they never would have won the raft in the previous day's challenge, either. Carter gave the thing a push, jumped on board, and picked up a bamboo paddle.

"I hope we're going the right way," Jane said.

"It's the only way that makes sense," Vanessa said. "Whoever took Buzz needs to keep heading east, just like everyone else. And we're the only ones with a raft. They'll have to go the long way around the bay, on foot. With any luck, we can get there before they can, and then we can cut them off."

"What do you mean, 'whoever took Buzz'?" Carter asked. "Chizo did this, and you know it."

"We *don't* know that. Not for sure," Vanessa said.

"Maybe you don't, but I do," Carter said.

Just the mention of Chizo's name made him burn a little hotter. He dug in with his paddle now, punching at the water as they set out for the other side.

Chizo had probably been planning this all along, hadn't he? Looking back now, it made sense. No wonder he'd made such a big deal with the tribe elders about allowing the outsiders—Carter, Jane, Vanessa, and Buzz—to compete in *Raku Nau*.

Chizo, they'd been told, wanted to be chief of the Nukula one day, like his father. And what better way of proving himself than by decimating the outside competition? He'd pulled them into the race, then he'd made it difficult for them from the very start—kicking gravel down through the slot canyons, pushing Buzz off a high ledge, even stealing bananas from Mima.

Now, he was taking it to a new level. By kidnapping

Buzz, he was doing everything he could to make sure they never finished, for sure. It wasn't even a question. Carter had known kids like Chizo all his life, in every sport he'd ever played.

Heck, I am *one of those kids,* he thought. *Takes one to know one.*

So if Chizo wanted competition, fine. He was going to get it. And he was going to be sorry he ever asked for it in the first place.

"How fast do you think we can get across?" Vanessa asked. She and Jane had already started flutter-kicking off the back of the raft for more propulsion, while Mima and Carter paddled at the front.

"Not fast enough," Carter said, bending to it. "Never fast enough."

Jane squinted into the sun. It had just begun to rise over the line of green jungle on the opposite side of the bay, straight ahead. Beyond that were the spiked peaks of Cloud Ridge in the distance. The ridge was called *Mayamaka* in the Nukula language, and it waited for them like a giant finish line against the sky.

As always, she took it all in, recording the details in her mind. The camera she'd brought from home was long gone. Even the paper journal she'd kept on Nowhere Island had burned up in a shelter fire. The best she could do now was to tell herself the story and commit it to memory.

July 14. Day 3 on Shadow Island.

Thirty-two runners set out from the Nukula village at the start of *Raku Nau* yesterday. Four didn't find their way to camp last night. That means twenty-eight of us are left. Sixteen will get to Cloud Ridge in time to earn the *seccu*, which is the winner's necklace. Only the runners with the *seccu* are allowed to cross Cloud Ridge to the east shore of the island. That's where the closing ceremony happens.

It's also where we need to get to, more

than anything. Ani, the only other person who speaks English here, said so. Sort of. Ani is an outsider, like us, but he's lived here most of his life. His loyalty is to the Nukula, but I can tell he likes us and wants to help. All he really said was that the tides on the east side of the island are the only ones we could ever ride away from this place. After that, maybe we could be spotted by a rescue plane, or a ship.

But first, we have to find Buzz. Period. Nothing else can happen if we don't do that. I'm hoping, hoping, hoping we find him soon. Otherwise, I don't know what's going to happen.

"How are you doing, Jane?" Vanessa asked, kicking alongside her in the water. "You look about a million miles away."

"I'm okay," Jane said. There was no reason to admit she was scared. They were all scared. They were all tired—and hungry, and homesick, too. She just needed to keep going, and to keep up.

"You're doing great," Carter said, looking back from the front of the raft. "Just don't stop. . . ."

But his voice trailed away as he looked past Jane toward the shore they'd left behind.

"What is that?" Carter asked.

"What's what?" Vanessa said.

When Jane checked over her shoulder, she could see the palm frond mats they'd slept on, and the dark spot in the sand where they'd built a campfire. But there was no sign of anything unusual.

"Over there!" Carter pointed to the place where the enormous bay gave way to the open water of the Pacific. And where the shoreline curved away and out of sight, Jane's eyes fell on a small figure: Chizo.

He was halfway up the trunk of a palm tree, where it curved out over the water. Clearly, he was trying to be seen.

"What the . . . ?" Carter said.

Already, Mima had begun to back paddle and speak in rapid Nukula.

"What's he doing?" Jane asked, as Mima quickly

maneuvered the raft one-eighty on the water. Chizo was shouting, that much she could tell, but the distance was too great to hear anything.

Then Chizo pulled something from behind his back and started waving it in the air. Jane's heart dropped at the sight of it. If there had been any doubt about who was behind all this, it was gone now.

Because the thing Chizo had in his hand was Buzz's tattered blue T-shirt.

CHAPTER 3

Buzz screamed out the second he saw them. Carter, Vanessa, and Jane were on the raft, heading straight toward him. Mima, too. It was good to know she'd stuck with the team. His blood seemed to run faster now.

"HEY! I'M HERE!" he shouted. Chizo had him tied to the tree, so the others might not see him through the brush, but Buzz waved with his bound hands the best he could. "COME ON! HURRY!"

His voice wasn't much more than a dry croak. There had been very little to eat or drink since *Raku Nau* started, and nothing since the previous afternoon.

None of that seemed to slow Chizo, though. As soon as the others had turned the raft around, he dropped from the tree and started west again at a fast clip, dragging Buzz along with the vine leash between them.

"At least give me my shirt back," Buzz said. Chizo said nothing.

Buzz kept his eyes on the ground, trying not to trip or stumble. He could feel the familiar dizziness that came from dehydration, and the last thing he needed now was a bad fall.

For a moment, his exhausted mind drifted into a daydream. He was home in Evanston, sitting on the basement couch playing a video game. Except this one was called *Raku Nau*. He was starring in his own game, and this was just another level he had to figure out. Another challenge. Another puzzle. These things always had answers. There was always a way out—

Chizo jerked him back to attention with a yank on the vine.

"Ekka!" Chizo barked at him. *This way.*

They'd come to a wide brook that flowed out of

the forest. Chizo cut inland. His head pivoted back and forth as he led Buzz upstream. He seemed to be looking for something, but what?

More important than that, Buzz wondered, what was *his* own best move right now? That was the question he would have asked himself on the couch at home. So why not here, too?

Almost right away, an answer popped into his head. With the others racing to catch them, he needed to do whatever he could to slow Chizo's progress.

Buzz dropped. He buckled at the knees, then lay all the way down in the running water. Not only would that make it harder for Chizo to pull him by the wrists, but it meant getting a drink, too. Already, Chizo was yelling. Buzz stayed where he was, letting the stream flow right into his mouth as he took swallow after cold, refreshing swallow.

Even that was a risk. They'd found out the hard way how dangerous contaminated water could be, but he couldn't stop himself from taking the chance. He needed the hydration as much as he needed to get in Chizo's way.

It didn't last long. Chizo easily had the strength to haul Buzz back onto his feet. He hooked his hand under Buzz's arm and started walking again, more deliberately than ever. Still, it was worth the quick delay. The water coursed through Buzz's insides like a shot of liquid energy.

Soon, they came to a shady alcove where the brook cut left. Several small banyan trees grew here, like the ones in the Nukula village. Their exposed roots jutted out from the trunks like table legs.

Chizo put a hand on Buzz's shoulder and pushed just hard enough to sit him flat on the ground, his back against the tree roots. Then he wound the long end of the vine around Buzz's chest, in and around the roots, and back again, securing him to the spot.

Buzz bucked and twisted, but Chizo was too powerful, and the vine was as strong as rope.

"You done?" Buzz said once Chizo had tied off the end of the vine. It pressed into his chest, making it harder to breathe, but he gave Chizo what he hoped was a defiant look. "You can go now. Okay?"

Chizo only smiled. His face was covered with gray-green river mud—the same stuff Mima had given Carter for the cut on his hand. It coated his skin and his hair, which hung in clumps down to his shoulders. He looked like a menacing human statue.

He didn't leave, either. More of the same vines hung all around the clearing, like odd party streamers, and Chizo pulled two down while Buzz watched. Next, he chopped the vines with a sharp rock from the stream, creating shorter sections of ten or twelve feet. He used one of those to tie off Buzz's ankles while Buzz sat helpless, his back to the tree and his feet stuck out in front of him. It was infuriating and humiliating, both.

"You're going to be sorry," Buzz said with as much venom as he could manage. His voice cracked when he said it, and Chizo only laughed. Then he pulled out the tattered blue T-shirt again.

"What are you doing?" Buzz asked as Chizo bent near. "Give that back!"

But there was no stopping him. A moment later, Chizo had tied the shirt around Buzz's eyes. All Buzz could see now was a blur of blue cloth. His panic started to rise.

"Leave me alone! Just go already!" he shouted. The only thing he had left to fight with was his voice, and even that effort left him panting for breath. Not being able to see made it that much worse.

He could hear Chizo moving around now. There were more cutting sounds, and a soft chafing, and things being dragged all over the clearing. He was up to something, but it was impossible to see what it was, much less do anything about it.

The only thing that helped now was knowing that the others were on their way.

Hurry, Buzz thought. *Please, please hurry.*

Carter bent his head against the wind, paddling as hard as he could toward the place they'd last seen Buzz. His brother wasn't the same video-playing couch potato he'd been two weeks ago, but that didn't mean he was equipped to take on Chizo alone. He'd need their help.

Three months ago, Buzz hadn't even *been* his brother. But then Carter and Jane's mom had married

Vanessa and Buzz's dad, and everything had changed. Carter hadn't exactly loved having new siblings at first, but that seemed like forever ago. The time on Nowhere Island had changed him. It had changed all of them. They were united now. Chizo needed to know he was messing with the wrong family.

"I don't know how, and I don't know when," Carter said, "but I'm going to make that kid sorry he ever met us."

"That kid is older than you, stronger than you, and taller than you. And so are his friends," Vanessa said. "I hate him, too, Carter, but we have to figure out a way to get Buzz and get back into this thing, or we're never leaving this island. Nothing else matters. Focus, okay?"

"Yeah, okay," he said, but he didn't mean it. He could no sooner block out his feelings about Chizo than he could turn around right now and give up on Buzz. It was all part of the same picture.

But Vanessa didn't need to know that. If Chizo wanted to mess with their lives, Carter would mess with Chizo's. First chance he got.

He dug in with the paddle again, but his arms burned, worse than the hardest football practices he'd ever had. The river mud Mima had given him for the cut on his hand was working, but his palm still stung. And even the seawater seemed to work against him, dragging like dead weight against his paddle.

"Car-tare!" Mima said. She glared over, motioning for him to watch as she took another slow, steady stroke, keeping her body bent low out of the wind. She was getting far more done with less effort, Carter saw.

A week ago, he might have been too stubborn to notice. Not anymore. Now he imitated her posture, and watched what she did until they were paddling together.

Soon, they began to pick up speed. Mima smiled. It wasn't something she did often, and it filled Carter with an extra rush of energy. He smiled back and felt his face flush. Even though his muscles wanted to quit with every stroke, he couldn't stop. And he definitely couldn't let the others down.

Not his sisters, not his brother—and not Mima, either.

Buzz listened from behind his blindfold, straining for any sign that Vanessa, Carter, Jane, and Mima were getting closer. All he could hear was the wind, the insect hum of the jungle around him, and the sounds Chizo made as he worked away.

What was he up to? What did he have planned? Right now, there were no answers, just wondering.

Buzz's mind was running in overdrive with all of it when a faint but distinct tickling sensation registered on his arm. It was a bug of some kind, and he shuddered, trying to shake it off.

Instead, the tickling sensation spread. He felt it on his leg now, too. And on his neck. It was like a soft vibration, getting stronger by the second.

Then all at once, the tickle was replaced by a sharp, stinging sensation at his elbow. Something had just bitten him. It registered like a flash of red in his brain.

Buzz squirmed against the pain. It was no good. The vines cut into his ankles, wrists, and chest every time he tried to move, keeping him firmly backed up against the banyan tree. He couldn't even touch the spot on his elbow. And all he could see was vague, blue-tinged light around the edges of his blindfold.

When another hot sting came up from his neck, it hit him. These were ants. Lots and lots of ants. No wonder they called it an army, because that's what it felt like.

He'd seen them in the jungle on Nowhere Island— great long lines of them, marching along a dead log, or over the ground. He'd even been bitten a handful of times. But that was when he could get up and walk away. Not this time. The realization came with a fresh wave of panic.

"Chizo, help me!" he yelled out. *"Please!"*

They were everywhere. He could feel them crawling along his arms, down his legs, up his shorts, even into his hair, where another rapid sting, sting, sting came up. It felt like someone had pressed the head of a hot match into his skull.

Even with the sweltering heat of the oncoming morning, Buzz felt a chill run down his back. This army of ants was in full attack mode, looking to conquer. And from where he sat, bucking and yelling for help, it seemed to Buzz that they were winning.

In fact, it felt like they were devouring him.

CHAPTER 4

Vanessa was first off the raft when they finally reached the shore. She splashed through knee-high water and sprinted up onto the dry sand and rock at the island's edge.

"Buzz!" she shouted. "Are you here? Buzz?"

Please answer, she thought. Even with the million things they needed to accomplish, there was only one thing she wanted right now, and that was to hear her younger brother's voice.

It wasn't just that she felt responsible for Buzz, either. They were all responsible for one another. As brothers and sisters. As a team. As a *family*. If one of them was down, they were all down. Their time in the South Pacific had driven that point home beyond anything Vanessa could have ever imagined.

Jane and Carter were there now, too, while Mima beached the raft behind them.

"BUZZ!" Jane yelled.

"HELLO?" Carter shouted. "WHERE ARE YOU?"

"Hang on!" Vanessa said, putting out a hand to silence them. "Do you hear anything?"

And then, there it was. Buzz's voice came back now, from what sounded like a good distance.

"Hey! I'm here! Help!" he said. Or more like screamed.

"Buzz!" she yelled back, and took off in the direction of his voice. It led her along a wide brook that cut into the forest. "We're coming! Hang on!"

Mima called after them as they ran. "What's Mima saying?" Jane asked.

Vanessa didn't stop to worry about it. She took one glance back and made sure Mima was following. That was enough.

"She can run faster than all of us," Vanessa said. "Don't worry. She's right there."

"It sounds like she's warning us about something," Jane said, but there was no turning back now.

Vanessa ran straight upstream, picking her way as fast as she could over river rocks and through several deep pools until, finally, she spotted Buzz up ahead. He was blindfolded with his own shirt and tied at the base of a banyan tree.

"Buzz!" she yelled.

"Vanessa! Help me!" he shouted back. He was jerking and spasming, almost as if there were an electric current running through him.

As Vanessa ran closer, she saw why. His skin was covered with tiny red-brown ants, crawling all over him. They'd swarmed in on Buzz from all around, and his screams said everything about what they were doing.

A sob escaped Vanessa's throat as she closed the final distance between them. She, Carter, and Jane scrambled up the low bank together, and across the clearing at a sprint.

"*FAH!*" Mima shouted once more from below. The word meant "no" in her language, but Vanessa was too intent on Buzz to respond.

Just steps away from reaching him, Vanessa's foot kicked something beneath the dead brush—something low and thick like a root in the dirt. In the same moment, a crude net of vines rose up, scattering the ground cover that had camouflaged it up to now. The net closed around Vanessa and caught Carter and Jane, too. As it did, Chizo descended from the tree over their heads, holding a vine in both hands, as though it were all on some kind of pulley system. Vanessa, Carter, and Jane fell into one another as the vine mesh pressed in from every side until they were completely enclosed in it, like a three-person mummy.

Vanessa struggled instinctively. Her feet and hands poked out through the gaps in the net, but the vines were as thick as her thumbs, and unbreakable. Carter and Jane were struggling, too. All three of them jumbled together, elbowing and stumbling, knees buckling. But the net was so tight around them, there was nowhere to go—or even fall down.

They were caught in Chizo's trap.

Carter eyed Chizo as he secured his end of the vine, running it in several circles around the tree and knotting it off. Vanessa and Jane were pressed in tight around him, all of them yanking at the net as they lurched and stumbled into one another. But there was nothing they could do.

Carter's mind burned with frustration. When they'd first arrived on Shadow Island, they'd all experienced the trapping skill of the Nukula. Vanessa had fallen into a deep pit. Carter had been nabbed in the water. Jane had been snatched right out from under Buzz's nose in the woods. It was no surprise that Chizo could rig something like this, but that didn't make it any easier to take.

"Are you guys okay?" Buzz shouted. "What's . . . happening?" He was tied to the same tree, just a few feet away but too far to reach. Carter could hear him gutting through the pain of the ant bites. Several red welts had already sprung up on his arms and legs.

"We're trapped!" Vanessa yelled back. "Right in front of you! *Chizo* did it. He got us, Buzz!"

Chizo slowly came closer, carrying a familiar,

crudely made spear. Carter recognized the long stick from the three black knots in its side. He'd sharpened it himself just the day before, and had forgotten all about it in the confusion of leaving camp that morning. Now, it was in Chizo's hand.

"That's mine!" he yelled. Carter reached through the mesh, but Chizo kept himself just out of range. The same cocky smile as always spread slowly across his face. He was enjoying this, for sure.

"Mima!" Jane said. "Please! Do something!"

Carter's attention turned to Mima next. This was clearly what she'd been trying to warn them about. She approached Chizo slowly now, keeping her own distance.

The two of them exchanged what sounded like harsh words. Mima took a step toward Buzz, and Chizo moved to block her.

When he spoke again, his voice softened.

"What's he saying?" Vanessa asked.

The whole time, Buzz was yelling out, and gasping in pain. It was impossible to stand there with any kind of patience. They had to get out of this—*now*.

"Come on!" Carter yelled, shaking the net with both hands.

"Omigosh," Vanessa said. "Wait. Is he . . . ?"

"What?" Jane said.

"I think he's trying to get Mima to leave with him," Vanessa said.

Carter stopped and watched Mima's face carefully. It made sense, if that's what was going on. It wasn't enough for someone like Chizo to put the four of them behind in the competition. He wanted to take away their only ally, didn't he?

And if it was true what Ani had told them—that everyone expected Chizo to be chief one day—then Mima might have every reason to take this chance while she had it.

"YOU GUYS, WHAT'S GOING ON?" Buzz screamed.

"Hang on, Buzz," Jane said. "Mima's going to help us—I know she will."

Carter kept his eyes on the exchange between Mima and Chizo. He hoped Jane was right, but the stakes were just as high for Mima as they were for anyone else. Staying behind now could doom her own chances in *Raku Nau*. It was hard to say that she owed them that much.

Chizo barked something out, as though he were losing patience. It sounded like some kind of order he'd given her. Mima looked straight back at him in a silent stare down.

Carter couldn't look away, either. He clenched a fist, just trying to hold on—and hoping for the best.

"Mima, do what you have to do," he said to her in English.

She turned then, and looked him in the eye. And even though she couldn't have understood Carter's words, her glance said everything. He knew what was about to happen. His gut told him so.

Mima wasn't going anywhere without them.

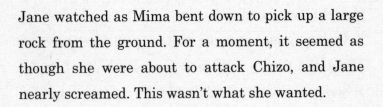

Jane watched as Mima bent down to pick up a large rock from the ground. For a moment, it seemed as though she were about to attack Chizo, and Jane nearly screamed. This wasn't what she wanted.

But then Mima turned and ran to where Buzz was tied up. As she started pounding at the vine that tied him to the tree, a sense of relief passed over Jane like a cool breeze.

Chizo yelled something in Nukula. *"Issa mekata, Mima!"* he said. *"Issa mekata!"*

The words echoed in Jane's mind. *Issa mekata.* What did it mean?

But Mima ignored Chizo. The last Jane saw of him, he'd turned and started back through the woods toward the shore.

"Is he going to take our raft?" she asked, suddenly realizing the possibility.

"Chizo!" Carter screamed. "Don't even try it!"

But he was already gone. He'd lured them all this way, and now he was going to steal their one advantage, leaving them in the dust.

"This is exactly what he was planning," Vanessa said. "I'll bet you anything."

"Except the part about Mima," Jane said. "He didn't get away with that."

Mima was still kneeling next to Buzz, and she had

just broken through the first vines. Buzz lurched away from the tree. He rolled in the dirt with his hands still tied in front of him, almost as if he were trying to put out flames. That's probably how it felt, Jane thought, with the ants still biting him all over.

His blindfold had finally come off, and Buzz's eyes met Jane's for a brief moment. He squinted through his own tears and seemed confused about what he was seeing. It must have been a strange sight, with them bound up in Chizo's net.

Already, Mima had moved to the other tree. She held the same rock over her head and started hacking at the vine that held the net in place. Jane felt it give way, but not more than an inch.

Mima shouted something that sounded like a warning as she gave one more chop. Just then, the net collapsed with all three of them inside. Jane hit the ground, still tangled up in the vines. Carter fell on top of her. His elbow caught her under the jaw as they landed, and her mouth filled with the taste of blood.

None of it slowed them down. The pain of a bitten

tongue was nothing next to what the welts on Buzz's arms and legs must have felt like. His face was pinched, and his breathing was fast and shallow.

A second later, Mima had dragged Buzz off the ground. Without pause, she started running him back toward the shore, speaking the whole time in her usual rapid-fire Nukula.

"What's she saying?" Carter asked Jane as they followed. Jane was the one who had picked up the most Nukula by now.

"Something about water," she answered. The word *"fania"* had jumped out at her. "Maybe the salt water will help with the ant bites."

"Or maybe she means we need to get that raft," Carter said.

"Jane, are you okay?" Vanessa asked, looking wide-eyed at her.

Jane swiped the back of her hand across her chin and saw the bright red smear of blood that had caught Vanessa's attention. Her mouth tasted salty with it.

"I'm okay," she said, wiping the rest of it away.

Back home, she might have cried, or at least stopped long enough to go into the bathroom, turn on the faucet, and rinse out her mouth.

Those days were far behind them now. If she said she was okay, then that would have to be good enough for Carter and Vanessa. And it was.

"All right, let's go!" Vanessa said, and they were running again, this time after Mima and Buzz.

CHAPTER 5

When Vanessa, Jane, and Carter reached the shore, Mima already had Buzz all the way into the ocean. She was rubbing the salt water over his arms and legs while he floated on his back, breathing normally again. His face showed some pain, but the water seemed to be helping.

Vanessa ran right to him. "I'm so sorry, Buzz!" she said, fighting her own tears.

"It's not your fault," he said.

"How are you?" she asked.

"I've been better," he answered, and gave a grim smile.

Between Jane's bloody chin and the bites all over Buzz's skin, they were all looking as beat-up as ever. But everyone seemed to have their minds on one thing now.

Chizo had taken the raft. Their hard-earned advantage was gone. They were farther behind now than they'd been at the start. And with the wind at Chizo's back, and the raft getting him straight across the bay while all the others went the long way around on foot, he would be able to come out of this ahead of the entire pack, or at least near the front.

There was no knowing where the other teams were by now, but it was clear to Vanessa that she, Carter, Jane, Buzz, and Mima were in last place. And if they didn't finish *Raku Nau* on time, there would be no getting off the island. No getting rescued. No going home.

It was an unacceptable thought. It wasn't even an option, Vanessa knew. There was no way they could let this stop them. They could tell Ani what Chizo had done, but by then it would be too late.

Besides, even Ani himself had said the competition was to be won "by any means necessary." Was this what he meant—by cheating and stealing?

Carter kicked at the ground several times. "I hate that kid! I really do!"

"What now?" Jane asked, pressing in close. All four of the siblings huddled together on the shore while Mima stayed in the water up to her waist.

"We have two choices," Buzz said. "We can start walking or we can start swimming."

"I say we swim," Carter said.

Vanessa didn't speak right away. It would be a scary-long swim for them, but it would also be a significant shortcut compared to going on foot.

She ran through the pros and cons in her mind. Buzz wasn't a fast swimmer, but then again, none of them had eaten. It was hard to know how much they could do in the water at this point. The cut on Carter's hand seemed mostly healed. That was a good thing. And while Jane was probably the strongest swimmer in the family, she also looked the most frightened at the idea of crossing the bay that way.

"There has to be a reason the others didn't swim it," Jane said.

"I don't think we have a choice," Buzz said, and nobody argued with that. "At least I'll get some more time in the salt water. That's got to be good for these bites." He had barely stopped itching since he'd reached the water.

"Mima! What do you think?" Vanessa asked. "Swim across?" She pointed to the water and made stroking motions with her arms.

"Or go around?" Jane asked, and pointed in a wide arc to indicate the curved shoreline inside the bay.

"Tazo," Mima answered simply. There was no discussion for her. Without another word, she turned to face the water, dove, and started across.

"I guess *tazo* means 'swim'," Jane said nervously.

It didn't matter anymore. The decision had been made. Mima had stuck with them this far, and she'd just done more than any of them to save Buzz. They owed her everything.

No way they could turn their backs on her now.

Carter was first into the water behind Mima. It was

colder than he'd expected, and the lack of fuel in his belly made it worse. Every temperature change here seemed to pass through him like wind through a screen door.

They'd swum in the ocean dozens of times back on Nowhere Island. Still, it never got easier. This wasn't open water, but the bay was wide enough to get some significant chop from the winds off the Pacific. The waves here were relentless, pushing them up and pulling them down, over and over.

To make matters worse, every time Carter lifted his head, he could see Chizo increasing his lead. There was no contest. Before they'd even put a dent in the swim ahead of them, Chizo was long gone.

The other question was whether Chizo had a plan for hooking up with his team, or if *Raku Nau* had already turned into an individual competition. It was hard to imagine Chizo as the loyal type. Eventually, each of the Nukula runners would have to figure out how to secure one of the sixteen *seccu* for him- or herself. It was just a matter of when.

But it was different for Carter, Vanessa, Jane, and

Buzz. They had to make sure each one of them earned a necklace. Ani had said those who finished *Raku Nau* were treated to a celebration on the eastern side of the island, just beyond Cloud Ridge. It was the only spot where the ocean-bound currents were passable, and the only place where they'd have a shot at escaping.

But that was never going to happen unless all four of them finished.

No—not four, Carter thought. *Five*. They had to make sure Mima got her own *seccu*, too. For them, it was going to be a team effort all the way to the end.

As he lifted his head again to check on the others, Carter heard someone shouting. It was Jane. He stopped swimming and came upright, treading in place.

"I have a cramp!" Jane yelled, about ten yards behind him. She reached down to grab her leg, dropped beneath the surface, and then popped up again.

Vanessa and Buzz were coming behind, but Carter got to her first. He held her up as best he could, with an arm around her middle. At the same time, he took in an unexpected mouthful of salt water. It burned his throat as some went down. The rest, he spit out.

"How much farther do you think it is?" Jane asked. She looked around, probably searching for something to grab on to. If this were a swimming pool, there would be a sidewall, or a shallow end to swim toward. But there was nothing here. They should have brought a piece of driftwood, or anything buoyant, Carter realized. None of them had been thinking clearly. The lack of food, water, and real sleep was taking its toll—not just on their bodies, but on their minds, as well.

"You can do this!" he said. Over the last two weeks, Jane had been braver than Carter ever would have guessed she could be. But right now, he could see the panic taking hold. Her eyebrows knitted together, and her mouth quivered as she fought back the tears.

"Carter . . . I don't know if I can make it," she said.

"You have to," he said. "Somebody has to tell Mom and Dad the story."

"What?" she asked, confused.

"You heard me," he said. If he couldn't get through to Jane with sheer encouragement, then he'd give her a task. Something she knew she could do. A reason to survive. "You're keeping track of all this, right?" he said. "With your journals and stuff?"

Jane didn't respond. It was hard to tell what she was thinking, and it didn't matter anyway. There was nothing else to say. They had a long way to go, and his little sister had every reason to be scared. But he couldn't afford to let her know that.

"Come on, Jane. You just have to keep moving," he said. "Turn on your back."

There wasn't even room for sympathy right now. Talking wasn't going to get them anywhere. He hooked his arm in with hers like they'd done before—and like he could see Vanessa had already done with Buzz. Pairing up was another good idea he should have thought of before they left the shore. Only Mima swam alone now, a good fifty feet ahead of them.

Soon, they were moving again, on their backs. Carter kicked for both of them while Jane rested next to him. In a way, it was easier to swim like this. Watching the sky was less frustrating than facing the shore, which never seemed to get any closer.

Even then, though, the wide blue expanse overhead

quickly reminded Carter of something else they needed: a rescue plane. The last plane they'd seen had passed right over the island, and over the camouflage barrier that hid the Nukula village from view. Maybe it had carried their parents and maybe it hadn't, but one thing was for sure: Mom and Dad weren't going to give up looking for them.

"We're getting closer!" Vanessa shouted, loud enough for Carter to hear. Jane's breathing was still shallow, but she had begun to kick alongside him.

"What did . . . she say?" Jane panted out.

"Just keep kicking," Carter told her. "Don't talk."

Jane only nodded, to show she understood. Vanessa was trying to be encouraging, but one glance to the east showed Carter that they still had an impossibly long way to swim. It was hard not to wonder if they'd made a mistake, choosing to go this way.

But there was no turning back now—and no guarantee they'd get there, either.

As the fatigue took hold, all four siblings linked up and

swam abreast on their backs. Jane took Vanessa's free arm with her own, and they moved like a human raft now, taking turns—kicking and resting, kicking and resting. Nobody spoke anymore. It was as though the effort of getting there was the only thing that existed.

That, and the wishing for it to be over.

Mima stayed ahead the whole time, swimming for a while, then treading water and looking back before continuing on. It was amazing how calm she stayed, watching them without ever moving closer to help. It may have meant she didn't think they were in real trouble. Or maybe it was a mark of respect. Or both. *Raku Nau* was supposed to prove worthiness among the Nukula. Maybe Mima was allowing them to do just that.

When the shore finally came within striking distance, Jane felt an overwhelming surge of exhaustion. Her arms went from weak to useless. Every kick became an effort. She pushed on, not even knowing how, until eventually, the water was shallow enough to stand.

She found herself staggering, then crawling the

last few yards onto a short gravel beach, where she collapsed on her stomach. The rocky ground hurt where it pressed into her ribs, but that was nothing compared to the need to *stop moving* for a while.

For several minutes, everything seemed gray. Jane lay there with the others, somewhere between sleeping and conscious, not even sure how much time was passing. The idea of getting up and continuing on seemed impossible.

That was until she remembered how hungry she was. Her stomach felt like an actual hole, right through her middle.

Vanessa was the first to put it into words—what they were probably all feeling.

"I need food," she said. "Like, actually *need* it."

"Yeah," Carter answered simply.

The mention alone was enough to get Jane to lift her head. She scanned the beach now, looking for rocks at the water's edge where snails might have gathered.

She'd eaten more snails than she could count on Nowhere Island. They all had. But for Jane, they were the worst thing she'd ever tasted—even worse than the live grubs they'd choked down. Still, she thought, she'd be happy for a mouthful of those slimy little things right now—raw or cooked, it didn't matter.

Slowly, she sat up. Mima was standing near the edge of the woods, looking ready to keep moving.

"Mima?" Jane said. "Is there anything we can eat or drink? *Fania?*" That was "water" in Nukula. "Food?" she asked, motioning to her mouth.

"Ah-ka-ah," the girl said, and headed straight up into the jungle.

"Is she saying 'Yes, there's food'?" Buzz asked. "Or 'Yes, we need to find it'?"

"Ba-nessa! Car-tare! Jane! Buzz!" Mima barked out. Jane looked over to see her staring at them from just inside the tree line. Her eyes seemed to say, *I'm not doing this on my own. Get up and come with me, right now.*

"She ought to coach football," Carter said as he put out a hand to help Jane up. "It's like she never stops."

But Jane noticed he was smiling when he said it, too.

Someone has a crush, she thought. Besides, it was

true about Mima. Whether or not she was suffering, she always seemed so full of energy.

Jane looked up into her face now and tried to at least seem like she was ready to go. Some part of her didn't want to disappoint Mima.

"You're in my story," Jane said. She knew Mima couldn't understand, but it didn't matter.

Instead of an encouraging smile, or any words, Mima curved her hands into two fists, and then curved those inward to knock the flat of her knuckles together twice, all while looking Jane straight in the eye.

It was hard to know what it meant exactly, but Jane returned the gesture. She closed her hands, curved them in, and knocked her own knuckles together twice. In a strange way, it sent a rush of energy through her—a feeling of connection that told Jane she could do this, too.

And she knew then that no matter what else happened here, she would never forget Mima as long as she lived.

CHAPTER 6

Vanessa took a deep breath and stood up to go.

Right away, she put her hands back down on her knees and ducked her head. The swimming, the hunger, the thirst—they were all taking their toll. Everything seemed to spin around her. Her stomach roared around its own emptiness.

"You okay?" Carter asked.

"I'm fine," she said, and tried to shake it off.

It was amazing what passed for "fine" in a place like this. If she made a list of all the food she had consumed in the past fifteen days, it wouldn't fill an index card. Not even double-spaced. Feeling terrible was normal. Barely getting by was a way of life. Not wanting to take another step but taking it anyway was something that happened about a hundred times a day here.

The demands of "real life" back in Evanston seemed like nothing now. The whole idea of getting up early, going to school, and doing homework sounded easy compared to this.

Not just easy. More like heaven.

Vanessa stopped long enough to shake off the thoughts of home. They always just slowed her down. She'd think about home when she got home. In the meantime, she'd think about *Raku Nau*—and about getting off this island.

"Let's see what we can find to eat," she said. They still had a long way to go before Cloud Ridge, and they still had to catch up to the other teams. The best way to do that was to put something in their bellies first.

They moved up into the woods, where Mima had stopped again to wait for them. She pointed at a branch over her head, and Vanessa nearly cried at the sight of several small purple globes hanging in clusters along the limbs.

"Is that fruit?" Buzz asked.

"Can we eat it?" Jane asked Mima, pointing to her mouth. "Please say yes. Please . . ."

"Ah-ka-ah," Mima answered, returning the gesture. Then she pointed at Carter and flexed her muscles.

"She's saying it will make us strong," Jane said.

"That's all I need to hear," Carter said.

Mima continued to speak, but in words Vanessa didn't recognize. Her gestures were confusing, too. Was she saying they should wait, or that they should go ahead and eat?

Then she turned and darted off into the brush, still calling back as she went.

"What's going on?" Buzz said.

"She'll be back," Jane said, and Vanessa knew she was right. If Mima had intended to strike out on her own, she could have done it long ago.

"Breakfast time!" Carter said. "Jane, come here."

Carter put his hands together like a stirrup and leaned over for Jane.

"Hop up!" he said. Vanessa stood next to him, offering her shoulder for support as Jane rose in Carter's hands, high enough to reach the fruit on the limb overhead.

"They're soft. I don't know if that's good or bad," Jane said. Buzz caught two as they dropped and brought them up to his face.

"They don't smell like anything," he said. "But they're heavy."

The fruits had pocked waxy skin, like a lemon or a lime, but bigger and rounder. It was hard to know if the deep purple color meant they were ripe or not, but there was one way to find out. And Vanessa didn't imagine that the others were feeling any pickier than she was right now.

"Should we wait for Mima?" she asked, already knowing the answer. There was more than enough on the tree for all of them to eat. And they'd waited long enough.

Buzz ran a thumbnail along the skin of the fruit in his hand. "I think this could be easy to peel," he said.

"Or," Carter said, "we could just do this."

He plucked one from the bunch and poked his thumbs right in, pulling it open with a soft wet sound. Inside, the fruit was pale yellow with a small bunch of tan-colored seeds in the middle. The flesh was thick and juicy, like a plum.

"Go ahead, Jane," he said, and handed it to her.

"Why am I going first?" Jane said.

"Because you're the bravest," Buzz said. It was worth a try, anyway. Jane usually couldn't resist any kind of dare.

Jane dug her fingers in and pulled off a moist chunk. The juice ran down her hand and over her wrist. She started to lick it off but drew back.

"It's *really* sour," she said. Then she started to put the piece in her mouth, until her face contorted again and she stopped. Jane had always been the pickiest eater in the group, at home and on Nowhere Island, too.

"I'll try it," Buzz said. He tore his fruit open like Carter had done and scraped a hunk of the flesh loose with his teeth.

Immediately, he spit the piece out. Not only was the fruit sour beyond anything he'd ever tasted, but it had a kind of dryness that sucked the moisture right off his tongue. It was a bizarre feeling, or flavor. Or both.

It was incredibly frustrating, too. Here they were with painfully empty bellies and a whole tree full of food that they might have to walk away from. Just getting up into the woods had been a struggle after their long swim.

"Mima eats these, right?" Vanessa asked. She'd tasted one of the fruits now as well. Carter, too. All four of them looked at each other, mystified.

"Yeah, well, Mima practically flies through the trees, and we can't do that, either," Carter said.

"Maybe she's used to them because she lives here," Buzz ventured.

"Maybe *we* just have to get used to it," Carter said. He tried another bite, but shook his head and spit it out a second time. "No way," he said. "That is the grossest thing I've ever tasted. Seriously. I'd rather eat grubs."

"We have to have something!" Jane said.

"Well, it's not going to be this," Carter answered.

"You don't mean that," Vanessa said.

"I don't see you eating it," Carter answered.

Their nerves were shot, Buzz knew. The more tired they got, the more they fell into the kind of constant bickering they'd done for months at home, before any of this began. But there had to be *something* they could eat.

As Buzz scanned the area, he saw Mima coming back through the woods. She was carrying something cupped in her hands. When she reached them, she looked at the discarded fruit on the ground, and then at their puckered faces, still working through the super-sour taste.

Mima burst out laughing. It was the first time Buzz had ever seen her laugh, and she seemed to be doing it *at* them, not *with* them.

"We can't eat these," Jane told her. She shook her head and made a face that showed how sour they were.

Mima only grinned. She obviously knew something

they didn't, Buzz thought. When she opened her hands, he saw eight bright red berries, each one the size of a jelly bean.

It wasn't much, but at least it was something. Everyone was too hungry to discuss it, and they took two berries each.

"Fah!" Mima said, stopping Buzz just before he tossed them into his mouth. She held up just one of her berries to show them. Then she put it on the end of her tongue and let it sit. Slowly, she began to chew. She was deliberate about it, and seemed to be spreading the berry around the inside of her mouth.

"What's she doing?" Buzz asked, but nobody answered. They just watched.

As she ate the berry, Mima's expression didn't exactly say *delicious*. She seemed to be working at it, and she didn't stop. Finally, she opened her mouth to show them. It was bright red inside—teeth, tongue, everything.

She pointed for everyone to do as she'd done. Buzz placed a berry on his tongue while Carter, Jane, and Vanessa did the same.

"This is worse!" Jane said, and spit hers back into her hand.

Buzz held his breath, determined to get through this. The berry had an intensely bitter flavor. He gagged once, but kept chewing, just like Mima had done. His body needed nutrition, and if this was what it took, then this was what it took.

Jane was the last to put her own berry back on her tongue, though she didn't look happy about it. Soon they were all coating the insides of their mouths and comparing their own crimson grimaces.

When that was done, Mima made a running jump at the tree where they stood. Her foot bounced her off the trunk, and she reached up to hang from the limb where some of the fruit still grew. With a fast swipe, she snatched another bunch of fat purple orbs and dropped to the ground.

It was all very confusing. The purple fruit was awful. The berry was worse. Their mouths were red as roses.

And Mima was smiling.

"It's no good!" Buzz tried, but Mima wasn't paying

attention. She rolled one of the fruits on the ground, maybe to soften it some more, and then easily peeled back its skin before taking a bite. Now, she chewed slowly, with her eyes closed. A bigger smile spread across her face, and she even sighed contentedly.

"I don't get it," Jane said. She shrugged her shoulders at Mima. "How are you doing that?"

Mima only nodded and took another bite.

Buzz still had half an open fruit in his hand, and sniffed it again. It still didn't smell like much, but when he touched it with the tip of his tongue, it was as though he were tasting a totally different thing.

The stomach-turning sourness from before had been replaced with a sweet explosion of sugar he couldn't explain. The sweetness ran right up his tongue, like a thirsty plant taking in water.

"You guys . . ." he said, then realized he didn't want to talk right now. He wanted to eat. He mashed the fruit open, scraping every bit of it into his mouth with his teeth, while the others watched, wide-eyed.

Quickly, they all joined in. Carter's eyebrows shot up, and a disbelieving smile spread across his face.

"That's crazy!" he said, looking at Mima. She laughed in return, as if to say, *Told you so.*

"It's like a magic trick," Jane said, her mouth full. "It tastes like . . ."

"Lemonade," Vanessa said.

"Yes!" Buzz and Carter answered at once. It felt as though they'd just broken into a candy store after two weeks of green coconut, snails, and bitter roots.

Everyone had two berries, and two of the fat purple fruits, which they quickly gobbled down. It wasn't exactly a meal, but the mood in the group had already shot up.

Buzz remembered this feeling from Nowhere Island—how even the tiniest bit of food could change everything when they were desperate. And this wasn't just any food. It was dessert! Which tasted like home to him. He felt tears at the corners of his eyes, but happy ones. For a few seconds, he could imagine sitting in front of a good movie, with a big bowl of candy in front of him, and nowhere to be, ever again, except right there . . . right at home, with Mom and Dad. . . .

The fantasy was like a bubble. Once he started, it

was hard to stop. But they had to focus. They had to keep moving. Again.

Before they turned to go, Carter grabbed two more of the fruit from the tree and ate them down quickly—just before Mima shouted out.

"Fah!" she said, but it was too late.

"What? They're good!" Carter said.

Mima held up two fingers emphatically.

"I think she's saying you should have eaten only two of them," Vanessa said.

"Yeah, well, too late!" Carter answered.

Buzz knew what he meant. It was hard to be sorry about eating when they'd had so little. Still, Mima had been pretty insistent. Now she shook her head and made a vomiting kind of motion, leaning over with her hands on her stomach—but then she laughed, too. It was hard to know how much she was joking and how much she was warning them.

Either way, there was no time for second-guessing. A minute later, they were headed uphill, away from the shore and once again toward Cloud Ridge.

CHAPTER 7

The next stretch of walking was a steep climb up from the bay through the woods. Carter kept to the front. He led alongside Mima as they crested a hill and hurried back down the other side—only to hike up another slope. Then another after that. It was as if the earth folded in on itself here, with a succession of ridges that grew higher as they moved farther away from the ocean. At the top of each hill, they found themselves looking across another tiny valley to the next ridge ahead.

It was rough going after the morning they'd had. It meant covering lots of ground without actually moving very far east at any kind of speed. The earth grew muddier, and it made for slick, frustrating climbs and descents.

The roots sticking out of the steep slopes made good handholds, but they could come loose without warning. More than once, Carter lost his footing and slid back the several yards he'd just worked so hard to climb.

The fruit was something in their bellies, but Carter was thirstier than ever now. And he didn't feel as full, or as good, as he would have liked. His stomach was tight, and cranky. That's what Mom used to call it: *cranky stomach.*

Near the top of the fourth rise, his insides began to clamp down. A sharp pain in his gut doubled Carter over, making it hard even to walk. He put his hands on his knees to keep from dropping to the ground.

"Carter?" Vanessa asked, coming up behind.

"My stomach," he said. "It feels like something's trying to eat its way out."

"I've got a little bellyache, too," Vanessa said.

"Yeah," Buzz said. "Me, too."

"It's that fruit," Jane said. "It tasted sweet, but it

wasn't. It's like we just ate a bunch of lemons on an empty stomach."

"Or a bunch of acid," Buzz said.

"Exactly," Jane said. "And Carter, you had the most. That's what Mima was saying about just having two—"

"Don't talk about it," Carter said. He took a breath and forced himself to stand. Up ahead, Mima had paused on the next crest to wait for them. When she glanced down at Carter, she seemed to fight back a smile.

"Car-tare?" she said, pointing to her stomach.

"Yeah," he said. *"Ah-ka-ah.* Not feeling so good."

She spoke some more, motioning with her finger down her throat and then back to her stomach.

"I think she says you should throw up," Jane told him.

"Yeah, no kidding," Carter said. "Great—just great."

He'd been sicker than anyone up to now, after drinking contaminated water on Nowhere Island. The prospect of anything like that happening again made him want to cry. He tried to swallow back the knife-like feeling in his gut.

"Just get it over with," Vanessa said. "You'll feel better if you do."

"That . . . is so gross," Buzz said. "You want him to stick his finger down his throat? I wouldn't do it, Carter. You're better off feeling sick and keeping that food in your belly. It's the only fuel we've had all day. Who knows when we're going to get anything else?"

"Would everyone please just stop talking?" Carter said. "I want to keep moving." The worst part was having everyone looking at him, and knowing he'd messed up. No way was he going to let that slow the whole team down.

Jane and Mima took the lead now, and they pressed on to the top of the slope in front of them.

"Look!" Jane said from up ahead. "Can you guys see that?" Buzz and Vanessa hurried toward her while Carter came slowly on, one foot in front of the other.

"Mayamaka," Mima said.

And as Carter reached the top, he saw Cloud Ridge, much closer now than he would have guessed. There were still miles to go, and then a climb up to the mist-shrouded ridge itself, but they were making progress. Even if it didn't feel like it.

Carter dropped to one knee, trying to breathe slowly. Even that effort put a painful pressure on his stomach. The third and fourth pieces of fruit had been a huge mistake. It was miserable and embarrassing, both.

"What do you want to do, Carter?" Vanessa asked.

His gut churned like it wanted to turn inside out. "I don't think I have a choice," he said, doubling over again. "Just go. I'll catch up."

"No way," Vanessa said. "Nobody's going anywhere alone. Not after what happened to Buzz."

"Well, at least don't look!" he said, just as it started to come up. His eyes watered, and his throat burned as his belly emptied itself out. The feeling was awful, and the taste was worse. But all Carter could think about was losing the one meal he might get that day.

When he could finally look up again, everyone had turned away, including Mima. He spit on the ground several times and took a deep breath. His stomach felt better. Not great, or even anything like good. But at least he could keep moving now.

At home, when you threw up, you got to lie on the couch and have flat soda. In this place, after you got sick, you got to climb another steep muddy ridge in the humid, mosquito-infested jungle, with nothing to drink.

"Do you need a minute?" Jane asked.

"Don't slow down for me," he said. "I'm right behind you."

Carter gritted his teeth, crested the next slope, and started down again, toward the valley floor below.

"What's that?" Buzz asked. He pointed across the narrow valley from the hillside they'd just begun to descend. It was tighter here than any of the previous side-by-side ridges.

There, on the opposite slope, was one of the other *Raku Nau* teams. Not Chizo's. Some other group— two boys and two girls. Jane recognized them from before.

This was good news. The team hadn't lost as much ground as Jane thought. At least there was that.

Every setback was hard to take—but every boost meant they were a tiny step closer to reaching the far shore, the ocean beyond, and, with any luck, Mom and Dad.

"Mima, is there any kind of shortcut?" Jane asked, motioning across. "Any way to go faster?"

"*Shor . . . cut?*" Mima said.

Jane picked up a stick and drew thick lines in the mud—one peaked ridge, then the next. She drew a line directly from the top of one to the other.

"That doesn't make any sense," Carter said. "You want us to fly across?"

But Mima took one look at the drawing and grew excited right away.

"*Ah-ka-ah!*" she said. She either knew just what Jane meant, or it had given her an idea. Either way, she was off and running again. This time she didn't move up- or downhill, but sideways, across the ridge where they stood.

"What's she doing?" Buzz asked as they started to follow.

"I don't know," Jane said. "Something good, I'll bet."

By the time Buzz and the others caught up to Mima, she was already climbing one of the many trees that grew out of the steep slope. She stood on a low limb, waiting for them. As they looked up at her, she spoke slowly, but still in Nukula. With her words, she added gestures. They were all becoming better at communicating using their own kind of sign language.

Mima pointed farther up the tree, which grew thin and willowy near the top. Her hand made an arcing shape until she was pointing at the opposite slope. Directly across, a scruffy palm grew almost sideways out of the hill. It made for the shortest possible gap between the two sides. But still, Buzz thought, if he understood her correctly, she was suggesting something crazy.

"Does she mean what I think she means?" Carter asked.

"Yeah," Jane said. "I think she does."

If there was one place they'd seen where a bending

tree could take a passenger straight across, this was it. Too bad it seemed just about impossible.

"We can't do that," Buzz said.

"Sure we can," Jane said. "If Mima thinks so, then I do, too."

It wasn't any comfort. The Nukula had all spent a lifetime learning to travel from tree to tree and to use the forest in ways Buzz had never even dreamed of. And Jane was a natural climber. Not like him.

"Mima!" Jane called up. "*Ah-ka-ah!* Do it! Show us." She motioned in the same pattern that Mima had made with her own hands, pointing to the waiting palm on the far side. It looked to Buzz like one-half landing pad, and one-half very bad idea.

"We've done harder things than this," Jane said. "The tree bridge on Nowhere Island was much farther across. This is only like twenty feet."

"Yeah, tree *bridge*," Buzz said. "It connected on both sides. All we had to do was walk over it—until it fell and nearly killed me."

"Don't be so picky," Jane said. It was supposed to be a joke, Buzz could tell, but nobody was laughing.

Meanwhile, the other team ahead of them had reached the opposite crest and stopped there. They seemed to be watching, to see what Buzz and his team would do.

"For all we know, those guys are the last ones except for us," Carter said. "I say we go for it."

"You don't have to impress Mima," Buzz blurted out. "She's not your girlfriend, and if we get out of here, she never will be. You know that, right?"

"Whatever," Carter said, reaching up to start climbing. "If you're scared, don't take it out on me."

"Car-tare! Fah!" Mima said. *"Mima . . . Car-tare . . . Ba-nessa . . . Jane . . . Buzz!"*

"I think she's saying we should go one at a time," Jane told the group. "Let's see what she does, and then we can do it after her."

Nobody questioned the idea anymore, and Buzz kept his mouth shut. He'd cost the group too much time already.

There was nothing to do now but watch, learn— and pray.

CHAPTER 8

Carter watched Mima closely, studying every move.

She took a deep breath and climbed several feet higher in the tree. It seemed as though even she was nervous, which scared him and made him want to protect her at the same time.

This was a risk, yes. But it was also an opportunity. If all twenty-eight competitors were still on track, they were going to have to reach Cloud Ridge ahead of twelve others. This move could save them a good hour, if it worked, and that could put them right back in the running. Every little bit helped now.

The other team on the far ridge hadn't continued on yet. They were still speaking among themselves, with their heads close together. But Carter couldn't worry about that, or where Chizo was, or anything else right now. This next task needed his focus.

The tree Mima had chosen was more than tall enough for the twenty-foot crossing. The problem would be if any of them fell on the way over. That would mean a drop of fifty feet or more, to the bottom of the valley below them. Nobody could walk away from a fall like that.

"This is crazy," Buzz said behind Carter, but even he didn't suggest they stop what they were doing.

Mima had reached the upper part of the tree in her usual quick time. Now she seemed to be testing the trunk where it thinned out. She'd need a spot that was flexible enough to bend a good distance, but not so thin that it would break off as she went.

Once she'd settled on a position, she started shifting her weight back and forth to get the tree rocking. As it bent away from the gap, she leaned in that direction, holding on with both hands and her feet pressed against the trunk. On the reverse swing, she pivoted around to pull it out over the space between the two slopes.

Carter shouted out. *"Fah!"* he said. *No!* The tree hadn't swung far enough to make a jump to the other side. Mima seemed to sense it as well and pulled back again, then forward a second time as they watched.

On this swing, the willowy tree picked up some momentum. It curved out and bent nearly sideways with her weight, until it was right over the waiting palm on the other side.

"She's got it," Vanessa said, just before Mima let go. She dropped for a silent moment, and then landed with a rustle and a crash in the crown of the other tree.

Carter noticed the way she drew in as she flew through the air and then splayed her arms and legs wide to catch as much of the palm as she could. It was an amazing trick, but not impossible.

Now it was his turn.

He shinnied up the narrow tree, aiming for a spot near the one Mima had used for her own takeoff. He was probably a little heavier than her, and he needed to be careful about snapping the tree as it swung.

As he left the ground behind, he could feel the tree start to sway under his weight. It was a delicate balance and already scary. Mima gestured at him to climb just a little higher, which he did. She stayed where she was in the crown of the palm—waiting to catch him, he supposed. Even now, he wanted to impress this girl, especially after the embarrassment of puking up the fruit she'd warned him not to eat. But he couldn't hide his nervousness. Hopefully, Mima wouldn't notice his shaking hands.

"You ready?" Vanessa called up.

"Yeah," Carter said, because there was nothing else to say. He pressed his feet against the trunk, bent his knees, and put all his weight into pulling the tree away from the gap, just like Mima had done.

On the first swing out, his empty stomach swooped with a nauseating wave. His breath seemed to rush out of his lungs, and a flush of terror came over him. It was like some kind of carnival ride, but not one he wanted to be on.

No stopping now, though. He shifted again, swung

back toward the slope, and put everything he had into the second swing out.

The opposite side seemed to rush at him. He stared into Mima's eyes like they were two targets, waiting until the tree seemed ready to snap back again—and then he let go.

For a second, maybe less, he was in the air—but it felt as though time had stopped. There was a *whoosh* in his ears, and then a violent, scratching crash of fronds as he landed. Mima was right there. Her arms wrapped around him, and she pulled him close before he could fall back, or out of the tree. His heart raced. For several seconds, he was just glad to have made it across, while his siblings cheered from the other side.

Then, just as quickly, his cheeks flushed. The closeness to Mima seemed to cut through everything else. They were tangled up in each other, face-to-face, inches apart. Carter knew he had to keep moving, even while some tiny part of him wanted to stay right where he was.

It was a stupid thought, he knew, and he hoped Mima couldn't see him blushing.

But he also imagined that maybe, just maybe, he saw her blushing, too.

She indicated for him to climb down through the fronds and make room for the next to come across. With the slope of the ridge beneath him, he wasn't nearly as far off the ground as he'd suspected. He pushed his legs through, grabbed on to the heftiest frond near the trunk, and dropped to the ground.

By the time he'd done that, Jane was already high up in the tree on the opposite side.

"You've got this, Jane!" he called out. "Just watch Mima and do like we did!"

As Jane got ready to go, Carter heard another voice somewhere behind him. He turned to look uphill and saw the other four Nukula runners again. They hadn't moved on at all. Now, they were working their way down the slope toward him.

And something told Carter they weren't coming to help.

"Carter! Watch out!" Vanessa shouted across. She

could see the other team hurrying toward the base of the palm where Carter stood.

"I see them," he said.

"What are they doing?" she called back. It was easy to imagine this had something to do with erasing the shortcut Mima had found. And right now, Carter and Mima were outnumbered. "Buzz, Jane—we need to go!" Vanessa said, putting a hand on the tree. In a few moments, the other team would be on top of Carter. And the palm on the far side looked just old and scruffy enough that four strong Nukula could knock it right out of the muddy ground.

"What do you mean? All three of us at once?" Buzz said.

"I think so," she said.

"Do it, all of you!" Carter called back.

Vanessa could see that he meant it. If she, Buzz, and Jane wanted to get across, it was now or never.

"Go, Buzz," Vanessa said. "Jane, go higher!"

Jane didn't wait. She was already climbing.

"You sure I should be next?" Buzz asked. A month ago, he'd weighed more than all of them. But now, he was getting downright skinny. He'd lost the most weight in this whole experience.

"I'm sure," Vanessa said. She was the heaviest now, and she would be the anchor.

"Stop talking and *climb*, you guys!" Carter yelled.

The two boys and two girls from the other team were swarming the palm, with Carter on the ground and Mima up above. Carter had his hands full. He couldn't stop all of them. Two of the others had begun to climb, and they started tearing away the fronds themselves, erasing the only landing pad Vanessa, Jane, and Buzz would have. Mima was trying to loosen their fingers from where they held on, but it was a losing battle.

Was this really happening? Another sabotage attempt? As *Raku Nau* got closer to the finish, the stakes seemed to be going up, and the competition was rising. Nobody was safe now.

Vanessa boosted Buzz into the tree and then pulled herself up. Maybe the tree would hold them, maybe it wouldn't. There was only one way to find out. And taking risks was turning into second nature here on Shadow Island.

No winning without boldness, Vanessa thought. She couldn't remember who had told her that. But she remembered something else—something that her social studies teacher had said one day. *The adventure you get is the one that you're ready for.* So maybe they were ready for this, right now.

And ready or not, here they came.

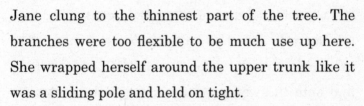

Jane clung to the thinnest part of the tree. The branches were too flexible to be much use up here. She wrapped herself around the upper trunk like it was a sliding pole and held on tight.

By the time Buzz and Vanessa had climbed up from below, the whole thing had begun to sway back and forth. It felt as though the tree might tip over at any second.

"Use that momentum!" Carter shouted. "You can do it! Now *pull!*"

Jane held on while Buzz and Vanessa leaned toward the slope behind her.

"And *push!*" Carter screamed as they reversed

direction and swung out, faster than she would have thought.

There was no time to think, and no need for a second swing. The tree bent farther than ever, until Jane was looking straight down at the top of the palm where they needed to land. Mima was still there, but so was the other team, pulling fronds away as fast as they could.

"Vanessa, go! Buzz, go!" she screamed, and they dropped.

At nearly the same moment, the tree snapped with a loud crack. Jane had no chance to let go at all. The breaking trunk did it for her. She fell straight down and onto the waiting palm, along with the broken tree itself. The other team scattered and leaped to the ground.

Buzz and Vanessa had landed a fraction of a second earlier. Jane crashed into Vanessa, and all of them kept moving as the fronds snapped away under their weight.

Jane reached, trying to grab onto anything at all. Her hands scraped over the rough palm trunk. It slowed her down a bit, but she hit the ground hard and rolled several times downhill. For several confusing seconds, it was a tumble of bodies, before she finally came to a stop.

And then, almost as if it hadn't happened, everyone was scrambling onto their feet again. Her rib cage throbbed with pain, and her legs were badly scratched. But more than that, she knew they had to get to the crest of the ridge and keep moving. They were in a race for their lives—and that was no exaggeration. Securing a necklace was the only thing that mattered. Otherwise, it was all for nothing.

The next thing Jane knew, she was clawing her way up another muddy slope. It seemed as though nothing could stop her now—until Mima shouted out furiously from somewhere behind her.

"Jane! Car-tare! Ba-nessa! Buzz!"

When Jane checked, Mima was standing still on the hillside, where a rocky piece of ground gaped open at her feet. The opening was dark. There was nothing more to see from here.

"What are you doing?" Jane shouted. She pointed toward the top. "We need to keep moving!"

"Ekka-ka!" Mima called out even more forcefully, and pointed at the ground instead. A second later, she'd disappeared into the black hole below.

CHAPTER 9

Vanessa was the first to follow behind Mima. There was no discussion among the family. They had to trust her and keep moving—period.

As she dropped onto an uneven rocky floor, she could barely see. Mima was just an outline, standing outside the small pool of light that spilled from above. They were in a cavern of some kind. At the far end, another jagged sliver of light showed the way out, maybe a hundred yards off. It was to the east, anyway, which was the direction they needed to travel.

"Come on down," Vanessa said, putting her hands up to help Jane with the jump. Carter and Buzz followed quickly behind, everyone still catching their breaths after the last five minutes of chaos.

"Are they following us?" Vanessa asked Carter as he hit the cavern floor.

"No," he said. "They kept going uphill."

"Good."

"Wow," Buzz said. "It feels amazing in here."

"Right?" Carter said.

The cool of the cave was like air-conditioning after the wet humidity of the jungle. Vanessa's sweat-covered skin was prickled with goose bumps. But it was a good feeling, like stepping into an air-conditioned store from a hot sidewalk on an August day.

"I hear water," Jane said.

"Me, too," Buzz said. "I guess we shouldn't drink it, should we?"

"No!" Vanessa answered at the same time as Carter. He knew better than anyone what contaminated cave water could do to a person's system, from that one awful night on Nowhere Island.

It was strange, the way their time on the last island was turning out to be a kind of advantage, Vanessa thought. It had been a true crash course in survival, for sure. But even more than that, the thirteen torturous days they'd experienced there had left her as determined as ever to make it home. There was no thought of quitting here, because it wasn't an option. Not after everything they'd been through to get this far.

"Everyone put a hand on someone else," Vanessa said. She could already feel Jane reaching up to rest a palm on her shoulder. "Buzz? Carter? Where are you?"

"We're here," Buzz's voice came from the dark. "I've got my hand on Jane, and Carter has me."

There was a sudden splashing ahead, and Vanessa jumped. But it was just Mima. She was already wading into the water, heading toward the far end of the cave. Mima never slowed down unless she absolutely had to. It was no wonder Carter liked her so much. She was just like him that way.

The water was icy cold as Vanessa stepped in. It came up to her knees, and she shuffled forward, feeling along the bottom with her feet, her hands held out in front of her. Something slimy rubbed past her leg, and a shiver passed down her back.

"What is that?" Jane asked.

"I think it's just a plant or something. Don't worry about it," Vanessa said.

"No," Jane answered. "I mean, up ahead."

Vanessa squinted through the dark. It was hard to see, but it looked as though they were walking toward a slight glow, coming from inside the cave. The contours of the rock walls around them began to show up as shadows, just slightly more visible than before. And the space around them took on a strange, blue-green color, almost as if it were lit by electric light. Which was impossible.

"What . . . is going on?" Carter asked.

"Mima, are you there?" Vanessa said.

Mima spoke back in Nukula, but there wasn't enough light for hand signals. She sounded excited, anyway—in a good way.

As they moved deeper into the cave, the glow brightened, and Vanessa began to see why. It was coming from the ceiling and walls up ahead. The rock there was lit with thousands of small points of light, like a universe of green stars over their heads. They cast enough glow to illuminate something that looked like clear threads beaded with glass, hanging down everywhere.

"What the . . ." Carter said, his voice trailing off in awe.

"What is this?" Vanessa asked.

"I think they're glowworms," Jane said. "And those strings are how they catch bugs, like in a spiderweb."

"Glowworms are for real?" Carter said. "I always thought that was just something in a song Mom used to sing when I was, like, five."

It was the strangest thing Vanessa had ever seen, and one of the most beautiful, too. The whole cave was truly stunning. It was as though this little universe had been created just for them.

There was something comforting about that. It felt safe, the way the glow held them there together in the cool air, staring up with green-glowing faces and not saying a word. Even Mima seemed to be enjoying it.

Outside, Vanessa knew, the night skies could be just as stunning. The stars over Shadow Island seemed to go on forever. But those always reminded her of how huge the world was, how wide the Pacific could be—and how lost the four of them really were out here.

That's why they needed to keep moving. It made no sense to linger here in the cave. All this staring in silence was a waste of precious time. And yet . . .

Maybe just another minute, Vanessa thought.

Just one tiny bit longer . . .

"We should get going," Carter said, after a long silent moment.

There was only so much standing around they could afford to do. In fact, they couldn't afford it at all.

"Mima, ready to go?" he asked. She'd been standing quietly but seemed to pick up his meaning when he spoke.

"Ah-ka-ah," she said, and turned to go. As she did, Mima stumbled and splashed into the water. Carter was right there, and he put out his hand to help her back up.

She looked at it for a second, her face glowing in the greenish light. It was a strange color, but still, she looked prettier than any girl he'd ever seen. Anywhere.

"You need a hand?" he asked. "Some help?"

Mima closed her grip around his, and he pulled her out of the water. She was lighter than he would have thought, and popped right up.

"Ratta," she said.

Ratta. It meant "thank you," he supposed.

For a moment, nothing happened, except for the feelings that welled up inside of him. His head swirled with thoughts about Mima, and about things that could never be—even if they were back at home.

How weird would Chicago seem to Mima? Probably just as strange as this place was to him. Would she be amazed? Scared? What would she think of all that concrete and noise? Or even cars?

"Car-tare," Mima said then. She reached up and seemed to scoop a handful of light off the cavern wall. Her fingers shone bright green as she spread the color around, and then held up two glowing handprints in the dark. It was like a magic trick.

"Awesome," he said.

"Ah-some," she said.

As she reached out to touch his face with the color, Carter couldn't help flinching a tiny bit. She made one stripe under each of his eyes, the way he might with football eye black. It was the same pattern he'd made on his face with dirt at the very beginning of *Raku Nau*, like his own warrior paint. He never would have guessed she'd even noticed it.

She gave herself two similar stripes then, and the feelings inside of him doubled with a warmth that matched the glow all around them.

"Carter, you coming?" Vanessa called from ahead. When he looked up toward the sound of her voice, he could see the other three, silhouetted against the jag of daylight at the far end of the cave.

"Yeah," he said, even though the last thing he wanted to do right now was step away from Mima, much less into the hot, sweaty, and buggy jungle outside.

But this wasn't a place that offered a lot of choices.

"*Ekka-ka*, Mima," he said. "Let's get out of here."

CHAPTER 10

Jane poked her head out into the sunlight. The sky seemed impossibly bright after the cave, and it took a minute for her eyes to adjust. She scooted across the rock table onto which she'd just emerged, making room for the others.

They were in a new and unfamiliar valley. This one was wider, with fewer trees, and Jane could see much farther in either direction to her left and right than in any of the previous valleys.

Straight ahead was yet another steep hill, but there was no reason to climb this one. The open grassy plain below curved down and around it, seeming to head for flatter ground in the direction of Cloud Ridge.

Vanessa slid next to her as Mima, Buzz, and Carter climbed out of the cavern, blinking in the sun. Carter had some kind of disgusting mash on his face, just under the eyes. Mima, too, Jane realized. It reminded her of the grubs they'd choked down on Nowhere Island.

"What's on your faces?" she asked.

"Nothing," Carter answered, wiping his away. He seemed embarrassed about it, and Jane didn't ask any more.

Instead, she held up her hands, indicating the two directions in front of them. "Which way?" she asked Mima.

But it was Vanessa who answered. "Down there," she said, pointing off to the left. "There's all kinds of bushes disturbed, and somebody has been chopping wood. It looks like they've started making camp. I bet it's for us. And I bet Ani and the elders are there, too."

That would make sense. They'd been greeted by the adults at the end of the first day and forced to compete in a grueling challenge before they could make camp. Jane suspected it would happen again, but she hoped not. Was it even the end of the day yet?

"What time do you think it is?" she asked. It was hard to tell, with the half cover of clouds overhead.

"Time to run," Carter said, and pointed up the slope behind them. "Here they come."

Jane turned to see the other team cresting the hill—the same one she and the others had just cut through, using the cave. Their few moments with the glowworms was going to have to pass for a rest break.

"This way," she said, and kept moving.

She scrambled down a nearly vertical rock face to the ledge she'd spotted from above. Then she sat down, dangled her legs, and made the jump to the soft ground below. Carter, Mima, Buzz, and Vanessa came right behind.

Jane could hear the other team as they worked their way down the slope, several hundred yards behind now. They were calling out as they came, maybe with some kind of taunting, she wasn't sure. But one thing was clear—the competition was still on.

As soon as her own team was on the ground, Jane started running again and didn't look back.

Buzz couldn't believe it felt good to run, but after the chill of the cavern, and with a sense that something else was about to happen, the adrenaline pushed him on. It wasn't food and water, but it was a burst of energy, anyway.

He was still the slowest in the group, and he worked hard to keep up. The downhill slope made for easier going. It was better than climbing, anyway. They still had plenty of that ahead of them, with Cloud Ridge looming ever closer.

Soon, they ran past the area Vanessa had pointed out. It looked as though some dry brush had been collected. Two freshly cut stumps spoke of the need for firewood as well. No sooner had they run by it all than Buzz saw the camp ahead.

Most of the other *Raku Nau* runners were already there. They sat gathered in groups around a single, large fire. Unlike the day before, this camp seemed to have been prepared for them. Some of the runners were eating. Others appeared to be sleeping. Those who had been there the longest had clearly had time for both.

Off to the side, Ani stood with two elders from the village. All three of them had been acting as some kind of observers, or officials, from the start of *Raku Nau*. They'd appeared at the beginning and end of the first day. And now here they were again.

Buzz's gut squirmed with anticipation as they all drew near the camp.

"Oh, man," he said. "The last time this happened—"

"I know," Vanessa said, with a twinge of dread in her voice.

The last time they'd been greeted at the end of the day, it wasn't just about making camp. There had been a punishing challenge waiting for them—the one that had won them the raft.

"Something tells me this isn't going to be easy," Carter said.

Buzz couldn't argue with that. Nothing about *Raku Nau* had gotten easier along the way. Just the opposite.

So what would it be now?

CHAPTER 11

Vanessa scanned the camp as they arrived. She counted nineteen runners. With the five on her own team, plus four more coming in somewhere behind them, that was twenty-eight in all. Everyone who had set out that morning had made it through the day. It was a pretty impressive accomplishment by all the competitors and a strong reminder that getting to the end was going to take everything they had.

Chizo was sitting with the four other boys who made up his team. For a moment—less than a second—his eyes widened. He hadn't expected them, at least not ahead of any of the others. That much seemed clear.

But he didn't spend any more time on it than that. A moment later, he'd gone back to the food in front of him.

None of the other runners paid much attention to their arrival, either. Everyone who wasn't napping was intent on eating. Each of them had a green leaf bundle, which seemed to hold some kind of steaming food. Back in the Nukula village, that was how they'd cooked meat, Vanessa remembered. Her stomach roared to life as she watched them shoving handfuls of it into their mouths almost as if that, too, were a competition.

Ani pointed them toward a spot by the fire as they came in. More leaf bundles were piled there, next to several waterskins on the ground. Most of the skins looked flat—which meant empty.

Vanessa didn't know what was inside the leaves, but she went for the water first. All of them did, including Mima. The thirst was overwhelming, and the signs of dehydration had become a familiar burden by now— the headache, the dizziness, and always, the painfully dry mouth and throat.

The first skin she picked up was empty. Not even a

drop came out of the open neck when she held it over her mouth.

"There's a little here," Carter said, handing one to Jane, but she gave it back.

"You found it, you drink it," she said. Carter started to object, but Jane had already turned away, scavenging through the pile.

"You should hurry," Ani said quietly as he walked past.

"Why?" Vanessa looked up at him. She had a whole list of other questions she wanted to ask, but not until they'd gotten something to eat and drink.

"Because the last ones are almost here," Ani said.

It didn't quite make sense, but there was no reason to doubt him. Ani hadn't lied to them yet, and when Vanessa looked over her shoulder, the last team was sprinting around the bend into sight.

Working faster, she picked up three skins at once and shook them. One had a sip of water at the bottom but the other two were completely full. She drained the small one even as she gave the other two to Jane and Buzz.

Jane drank too quickly, losing a good amount of water out the sides of her mouth. Buzz was like a machine. His head tilted back, and he drank without losing a precious drop, as though it were the sweetest thing he'd ever tasted.

Just as the last four runners arrived, the female elder stepped forward and called out with a long, trilling note. It was clearly a signal. Everyone around them responded as they had at the beginning of the first day and just before the previous challenge. They put down whatever they had in their hands, went to one knee, and placed one palm flat on the ground. Even the incoming runners knelt down, still heaving to catch their breaths. Those four had left camp that morning well before Vanessa and her team, she knew. They must have gotten lost along the way. Or maybe someone had sabotaged them, too.

Vanessa had another waterskin halfway to her mouth when the male elder shouted out a word she didn't recognize, but one that was obviously aimed at her. Ani was already there to take the skin out of her hand.

"Please?" she said. The small amount she'd had was like a tease more than anything. "Just let me finish that one."

But Ani shook his head. "Those who arrive earliest receive the most," he said. "Those who arrive later receive the least."

Ani ducked his chin, indicating the ground where Mima had already knelt. He waited until the rest of them had done the same before he went on.

Vanessa saw that the other runners were glancing around now. When she looked again, she realized they were all examining the trees surrounding camp. Many of them were painted with the familiar shades of brick red, black, and milky white, in zigzagging patterns, wavy lines, and symbols that may or may not have told a story. The colors were familiar by now. They'd been used to mark the *Raku Nau* course from the start. But the symbols were impossible to interpret.

Each tree held a large woven-leaf basket in its lowest limbs. From each of those, a braided cord hung down. At a glance, it seemed there was probably one tree and one basket for each runner.

"This will determine which of you will continue on toward Cloud Ridge," Ani told them.

"What do you mean?" Carter said.

"Five will end their journey here," he said.

"In other words—this is do or die," Vanessa said, and swallowed hard.

Ani's words were somehow a surprise, and not, at the same time. *Raku Nau* was a relentless competition and always changing.

The lingering smell of cooked meat didn't help, either. They'd barely had time to drink water. Now there would be no food and no rest before this next challenge began. The only ones who had it worse were the four who had arrived behind them.

"So, what do we have to do?" Vanessa asked. But before Ani could say another word, Carter let out a low growl.

Vanessa turned to see him looking at Chizo, who knelt on the other side of the fire.

"Issa tonna atzo—Car-tare," he called out, flashing his usual cocky grin.

"I'm going to wipe that stupid smile right off his

face." Carter said under his breath.

"But not now. Not here," Vanessa told him.

To her surprise, Carter nodded.

"I know," he said. "He's just trying to throw me off. But his time's coming."

Normally, her brother would have jumped at Chizo first and thought about it later. This kind of patience was a whole new thing for Carter. It looked as if he was finally learning to play the game.

They all were.

Carter listened carefully as Ani knelt with them and explained the upcoming challenge. He spoke in English while the other elders addressed the larger group in Nukula.

"The next phase of *Raku Nau* is beginning. You will choose a tree, in the order that you have arrived," he said. "Each one will hold the basket's cord over your head. If your arm drops, the cord will tear the weave and release the *atzo* inside."

"*Atzo?*" Jane asked.

"Blue paint," Ani said. "It signifies death. The end of *Raku Nau*. Red is the fire that began it. Blue is the color that ends it."

"That's it?" Carter asked, looking at the prepared trees around them. "That doesn't sound so hard."

"No. It is very simple," Ani said. "The question is, how long can you do this very simple thing? It is a test of the body, and of the mind."

"You said five people won't continue?" Vanessa asked.

"That's correct," Ani said.

Carter took a deep breath. Chizo would just love it if he blew this now. He had to focus. And he had to be strong, for himself, but also to help keep the others going.

"So we just have to last longer than five of them," he said. "We can do this, you guys."

"We have to," Jane said.

And, of course, she was right. He just hoped they could pull this off. Because if not, it would all end right here.

Buzz was twenty-fourth to pick his spot in the challenge. The elders had been watching carefully, and they had noted who arrived at camp ahead of whom. He'd been the last of his group to reach the fire circle, and the twenty-fourth overall.

That gave him a choice of five trees remaining. He went to each them and tried to figure out which offered any kind of advantage. It was nerve-wracking, not knowing what might be important here, or if he could do this, or how long the challenge would last. Most of the Nukula kids had all eaten and had a rest—not to mention, they'd all seemed stronger than him to begin with.

We only have to outlast five, he reminded himself. It wasn't just about endurance. One slip of the arm, and you were out. There was going to be some luck, as well as some strategy, to all this.

Some trees offered more canopy overhead, but the real distinction seemed to be the surface on which they'd be standing underneath. Those who had chosen first had selected stations with flat ground. Buzz was left to choose between large exposed tree roots or uneven rocky ground, both of which meant dealing with a tricky stance.

Finally, he picked a station with two large crisscrossing roots, mainly because it was closest to members of his own team. If he was going to be uncomfortable, at least he'd be able to see Carter and Vanessa from this spot, though not Jane or Mima.

Once he'd chosen, one of the elders came over. He indicated for Buzz to reach above his head and straighten his arm. Buzz did as he'd been shown, and the man knotted the cord into a loop where it hung to Buzz's wrist. Then he used a stone blade to cut the cord just beneath the loop.

That was how they equalized the competition, Buzz realized. Everyone's arm would be extended the same way, and each cord was cut according to the size of the competitor. It was the strain on each person's arm that would be the determining factor. Buzz could already feel the pain, and they hadn't even started.

"You got this, Buzz," Carter called over. "Put your arm down and rest until we have to start."

Nobody had said so, but it seemed like a good guess

that the next day of the competition would be its last—all about the final ascent to Cloud Ridge, where the sixteen *seccu* were waiting to be claimed.

Buzz thought about what would happen if they didn't all make it through this challenge. What then? Did they give up at that point? It was a scary thought and probably best not to dwell on it.

Ani walked from tree to tree as they got ready. Buzz used the chance of his passing to find out what he could.

"How far ahead did everyone else get here before us?" he asked.

"Enough time to eat and rest," Ani said.

Chizo had been the seventh to choose a tree, which meant he'd been seventh into camp. There was some small satisfaction, knowing that he hadn't come in first, after everything he'd done to them. Buzz's memory of his own capture was still hard to shake off. With any luck, Chizo would go down in flames on this challenge. Then they wouldn't have to worry about him anymore.

"Ani, this morning Chizo stole our raft," he blurted

out. "I mean, actually, he stole *me* first. Kidnapped me right out of camp. Then, when the others came after us, he took the raft, too. Is he even allowed to do that?"

Ani seemed unperturbed by the question. "If you allowed him to do it, then yes," he answered. "As I told you before, *Raku Nau* is achieved—"

"I know, by any means necessary," Buzz said. "But that doesn't seem fair."

Ani stared back at him, offering no further explanation. He hadn't even blinked at Buzz's story. It was one more reminder that life was very different here.

"What's Chizo's deal, anyway? Why's he such a jerk?" Buzz asked. "Nobody else is running *Raku Nau* the way he is."

"Chizo is like his father," Ani said quietly. "*Farka*. It means 'storm.' The Nukula believe these traits come from nature—from the trees and the earth. And they are passed on through the blood. *Farka*. It is Chizo's nature."

Ani had previously told them that Chizo's father

was chief. Everyone in the village expected Chizo to take that role one day. But that couldn't happen unless he did well in *Raku Nau*. Without a *seccu*, Chizo would have no chance of advancement in the tribe, just like anybody else.

"I have another question," Buzz said, but he was cut off. The two other elders had begun calling the group to attention. Once again, all the competitors came into their starting position, each at the base of his or her tree. Buzz did the same, pressing his right palm into the ground.

He took a deep breath and exchanged a look with Carter, who squeezed his fist and nodded, as if to say, *We got this*. When Buzz looked to Vanessa, she gave a nervous smile. But even that helped. Buzz was nervous, too.

The start of the challenge was a familiar process by now. The male elder stood near the fire in the middle of camp. The woman next to him let out another long, sung call, and as it ended, the man brought his hand down to his side. With that, the competitors all came up to a standing position.

Buzz took another deep breath, settled his feet as evenly as he could, and slipped his hand through the looped cord over his head.

The challenge had begun.

CHAPTER 12

The first fifteen minutes or so were harder than the second fifteen minutes. Jane was guessing at time. It took a while to find a good posture, and for her heart to slow down, as the challenge stretched on.

Occasionally, a drip of milky blue paint caught the top of her head, or landed near her feet, giving a clue of what was inside. Jane tried to keep as still as possible, leaving no chance of disturbing the woven basket above her.

Most of the people she could see did the same, with one hand straight up and the other arm bent over the tops of their heads. A few of the Nukula around her were more fidgety, never staying in one position for long. And yet, their upper bodies never wavered. It seemed unlikely they'd be among the first to get eliminated.

Jane didn't want *anyone* to lose a chance here, but it was complicated. If she, Buzz, Vanessa, or Carter made a mistake now, the whole thing was over. They'd either continue on from here as a group, or they weren't going anywhere.

She imagined what her parents would think if they could see this crazy challenge—twenty-eight kids in a jungle clearing, each of them with one arm held high, a paint-filled basket waiting to splash down on them if they so much as twitched. It was like a strange tribal version of a "time-out" that might happen back home for the really bad kids at school.

If only this were *just a time-out*, Jane thought. But the stakes were far bigger than no Internet for a week, or no recess. In fact, this was as big as could be.

A shout and a splashing sound came from somewhere nearby. It brought Jane's thoughts back to the forested arena where the challenge was taking place. She looked over and saw a Nukula boy dripping in milky blue liquid. His arm was down, and the basket over him had split open at the bottom. He shouted out a word Jane didn't know, then ripped the cord from his wrist.

"Jane!" Carter shouted over. "Watch it!"

Looking up, she realized her own hand had begun to droop. It was like being woken from a standing dream. She hadn't been asleep exactly, but when she realized how close she'd come to ruining everything, she snapped wide awake.

There could be no daydreaming in this, she realized. No thinking about anything except the challenge. One moment of lost concentration and it was all over. For everyone.

Buzz's arm was already starting to go numb. The throbbing he had felt in the first hour had given way to a dull, heavy feeling. It seemed to center somewhere around his shoulder, though he couldn't be sure because he couldn't feel much of anything. But he was still in this, and right now that was all that mattered.

Only one person had been eliminated so far. Four more to go. Most games or sports were scored by gaining points. It was simple. Whoever scored the most won the game. But points didn't matter in this challenge. Nobody was ever really ahead. So long as you were still in it, you had the same shot as anybody else. No matter how long it took.

Buzz adjusted his arm and told himself to settle in for the long haul.

It must have been a good two minutes more before he began to realize the signal his brain was sending from his stomach. Or, more accurately, from his bladder.

"Oh man, I gotta pee!" Buzz shouted. "Really bad!"

"You have to hold it," Vanessa said from her station.

Buzz was already struggling, his lower half starting to squirm.

"Buzz, don't wiggle. You'll break the basket!" Vanessa shouted.

"I drank way too much water," Buzz said, wincing from the pain. Now that he'd come fully aware of the need, it seemed as if waiting was no longer an option.

"Buzz! You have to stop moving. Right now. *Stop it!*" Vanessa told him. She had her bossy-older-sister voice on. He recognized it right away and knew what she was doing. She was trying to motivate him.

For a moment, it seemed to help. "Okay, I think it's going away," Buzz said.

He straightened up his body and started to get back some composure—but not for long.

"Oh-oh, it's back. It's worse. It really hurts," he said.

"So just pee!" Carter yelled.

"What do you mean?" Buzz called back.

"I peed on you when you got that stupid jellyfish sting. If I can do it, you can do it. Just pee. Right there. It doesn't matter," Carter said. It was strange to discuss it so openly, but nobody beyond Ani could understand them, anyway.

For a few seconds Buzz didn't say a word. He stood there, arm extended, trying his best to stay balanced and, at the same time, to relax enough to go in his shorts.

Just another day on Shadow Island, he thought, not even sure whether to laugh or cry.

"Are you doing it?" Carter asked.

Buzz gave no response. It was all he could do to juggle everything he had going on already. And then—

"Ahhh . . ."

It happened. The relief was stronger than any embarrassment ever could have been. To his own surprise, he didn't even care, now that it was done. It was like Ani had told them already. *Raku Nau* was to be won *by any means necessary*.

"Buzz?" Vanessa called out. "You okay?"

"Yeah," Buzz called back. "Much better."

"Told you so," Carter said with a laugh.

"Good job, Buzz!" Jane called from even farther off, as Buzz took a long, careful sigh of relief.

Another near disaster averted. They were still in this.

"Are we allowed to talk to you?" Carter asked Ani as he passed by. Ani was walking among the competitors, as were the other elders. They were monitoring the challenge, Carter supposed.

"You are free to make your own choices," Ani said.

Carter kept his eyes straight ahead, not looking Ani in the face. He needed information, but he needed to focus, too.

"Tell me about the eastern shore," Carter said then. "Are the tides all the same over there? Is one part better than another?"

"For what?" Ani asked. He stepped closer to put himself in Carter's eye line. His stare seemed to say, *Think about your answer.* Ani had done this from the start, doing what he could to tell them how to get off the island. His loyalty was to the Nukula, but he knew what it meant to be an outsider here, too. And Carter realized he needed to be careful of what he said.

"Just curious," he answered, returning Ani's gaze.

"Many Nukula come to the east shore for the *Raku Nau* final ceremony in outrigger canoes," Ani said. "The celebration that follows can go on for as long as two days."

In other words, Carter thought, *there will be boats there. And, maybe, a chance to slip away at night.*

"Didn't you say people guarded that side of the island, too?" Carter said.

"Yes. They do," Ani said plainly.

In other words, this wasn't going to be easy. The Nukula were as protective about outsiders coming in as they were about anyone leaving the island.

"One more question . . ." Carter said. He paused, unable to ask it.

Ani smiled ever so slightly. "Mima?" he asked.

Carter nodded.

"Stay focused," Ani said, and then walked away.

A second splashdown sounded from somewhere in the trees around them. Carter wasn't positioned to see who it was, and his heart jumped.

"Vanessa?" he called out. "Are you there?"

"I'm here," she called back. "I'm okay. Mima, too."

"Okay." Carter said, as much to himself as anything. He wiggled his fingers and moved his shoulder a tiny bit back and forth, working out some of the stiffness.

Two runners were out—three more to go before this was over. Or at least, before the next part could begin.

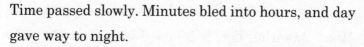

Time passed slowly. Minutes bled into hours, and day gave way to night.

As the sky dimmed, the fire in the middle of camp seemed to brighten. Vanessa wished she could feel the warmth of it. Not because it was cold—not yet, anyway. But because fire was one of the only comforts available to them out here. The light, the warmth, the security—it was a far more powerful force than she ever could have known, going about her old life in Chicago.

It was a fine line now between letting her mind wander and staying focused. The challenge had been on for at least four hours, she suspected. Maybe more. Her shoulder felt like concrete, and her hand tingled as she flexed and unflexed her fingers inside the loop over her head.

Two more had fallen out of the competition over the past few hours. Only one more to go. Chizo was still there, unfortunately. She could see him, standing tall and proud under his tree, his face mostly shadowed now with the dimming light.

Conversation from tree to tree had dropped down to an eerie silence. For a while Chizo had spoken to Mima, taunting her, it sounded like, from the tone of his voice. Vanessa had recognized the phrase he'd spoken with such venom after she refused to leave with him that morning. *Issa mekata.* She wondered what it meant, and she intended to find out.

Meanwhile, she was in trouble, and she knew it. When she flexed her dead hand, her arm jerked. The cord descended less than an inch, but she heard the sound of the basket rustling against itself, and a fat drop of blue liquid ran down her arm.

"No," she said, just to herself. Every part of her wanted to put her arm down. But Jane, Carter, Buzz, and Mima had made it this far. So would she. They just had to outlast one more person.

This was what Ani had mentioned at the start. The challenge was deceptive. Not only was her body rebelling against her, with cramps and numbness, but her mind was an obstacle as well. Every other thought had something to do with wanting this to be over. And there was no way to slow time down *more* than constantly wishing it would speed up. She'd learned that on Nowhere Island, too.

The trick back there had been to keep busy. Distract herself with work. Do anything that would pass the time, hopefully without her even noticing that it was going by. There was no way of knowing how much longer this challenge would continue.

But one boy under a nearby tree had definitely caught her attention now. It was like looking at a mirror reflecting what she was feeling inside. The boy's face contorted with the effort as he rolled his shoulder and tried to stand up taller. Vanessa could feel the tremors in her own muscles, and she could see the same thing happening to the boy.

His basket bowed just slightly at the bottom as he readjusted himself one more time. A teammate of his called out from nearby. The boy looked up, gave a sharp intake of breath, and then very slowly came to a full stop, like a statue in the twilight. The only thing that moved now was his trembling arm.

Vanessa watched him closely. He wasn't going to last much longer. She could feel it. This was down to the two of them.

"How're you doing, Vanessa?" Carter called over. His voice had been a comfort for the first several hours. They'd stayed in touch that way, but now it was everything she could do just to keep her arm from jerking, her shoulder from spasming. The effort of speaking was more energy than she could afford.

"Vanessa?" Carter called again.

"Not now," she said, in a fast gasp. If he heard her, she wasn't sure, but he didn't say anything else.

Mima was watching, too. Her wide eyes, focused on the basket over Vanessa's head, felt like a warning. Vanessa kept her own eyes on the boy across the way, waiting for his arm to give out first.

She would have thought that this showdown was all in her imagination, but others seemed to have noticed it, too. A voice came from across the clearing, followed by two more speaking the same words. She could tell just by the tone that some of them were yelling encouragement—probably to the Nukula boy, not to her. And some were yelling taunts. The energy around the camp had suddenly risen again. Word spread from tree to tree, and more voices filled the air around her.

Maybe this was all part of the challenge, trying to psyche out the competition. She was glad she couldn't understand the words she was hearing. It would have only made things more difficult.

It was hard to know how much more time passed. The sky turned to a deep blue-black, with patches of stars that showed through the clouds overhead. The sound of cicadas and other insects began to compete with the shouts that still punctuated the air. And with the bug noise came the bugs themselves. Vanessa knew she wasn't the only one with mosquito bites up and down her arms and legs, but still, every sting made her want to reach out and slap at her skin, which was the last thing she could do right now.

When the sound of ripping leaves and the splash of paint came out of the darkness, Vanessa's heart leaped. She looked over, and the boy she'd been watching was still there. She'd been expecting to see him dripping wet in the firelight, but the sound hadn't come from his tree, she saw.

A shout echoed through camp—Ani's voice—and all the other competitors came alive with movement and more shouting. And laughing? Yes, laughing.

It was over, but for whom?

Mima was there now. She was safe, that much Vanessa could tell. As she slipped her hand out of the loop and turned to find the others, her shoulder let up a silent scream of pain. It dropped her to her knees. When she tried to reach up and massage it, her other arm was dead, too. A painful feeling of pins and needles like nothing she'd ever felt before ran through her body, and she dropped back to lie flat on the ground.

"Carter!" she yelled. "Buzz! Jane! Where are you?"

The other competitors were moving around her, but it was hard to see in the dark. Faces flashed by. Whoops filled the air.

Mima reached down and helped her sit up. Still, the electric feeling of restored circulation in her limbs was painful.

"Where's Carter?" she asked Mima. "Jane? Buzz?"

"Jane," Mima said, and pointed as Jane appeared out of the dark.

Jane dropped down and threw her arms around Vanessa's neck. For a crazy moment, Vanessa couldn't tell if Jane was crying or laughing, happy or sad.

"Where are the boys?" she asked. "What happened, Jane?"

"They're like you," Jane said, with a clear laugh now as she sat back on the ground next to her sister. "They can't move! But they made it, Vanessa! We all did! We're going to finish this thing—together. Once and for all!"

CHAPTER 13

Buzz sat alone, staring into the embers of the fire, wondering if he'd ever get to sleep that night. They'd been given a small amount of food and water after the challenge, but it was hard not to wish for more.

The heat from the blaze had dried his shorts as well. Still, he was as filthy as everyone else, from climbing and descending all those mud-covered hillsides.

He remembered getting caught in a downpour one day, riding bikes with Vanessa through Evanston. Her back tire had spit water and mud all over him for miles. That had seemed like getting dirty, once upon a time.

Now, he realized, he'd barely known what tired, dirty, hungry, and thirsty really meant before all this. Nobody had even made sleeping mats for the night. It seemed that all the remaining runners were just as beat and were resting up for the final ascent. Carter, Jane, and Mima lay nearby, sleeping on nothing more than some quickly gathered dry grass.

Vanessa was speaking with Ani quietly, as they stood off together at the edge of camp. Buzz knew they should all be asleep, but his thoughts were on Cloud Ridge. From what he'd seen so far, the ascent was going to be the toughest part of this yet. It made him nervous in an old familiar way. He was changed, for sure, but he was still the slowest on his feet. How terrible would it be if they missed out on the *seccu* now? And what if it was all his fault, in the end?

The butterflies in his stomach that had started after the last challenge were still fluttering around inside like a swarm. He needed the rest. They all did. But it didn't seem like sleep would be coming any time soon.

Jane stared at the blank night sky, wishing for stars. There was something depressing about an empty, black sky in this place. At least when there were stars, it was something to look at—and something to wish on, too.

She could see Buzz sitting alone by the fire. He looked as deep in thought as she felt. Vanessa was still up as well, walking slowly around the camp with Ani. Carter and Mima were both deep asleep, on either side of her.

But for Jane, it wasn't so easy. She was always the last to fall asleep, her mind racing with thoughts and ideas.

This wasn't even close to over. The end of *Raku Nau*, if they made it, was only the beginning of what came next. That long night of tossing on the waves before they'd landed on Shadow Island was a reminder of just how difficult it would be once they got back out on the water. And who knew how long it would take to be spotted after that? A day? Two days? A week?

Jane shuddered, and she tried to think of something else. It wasn't easy. The closer they got to the end of this, the more she missed being home, and seeing Mom and Dad every day. She'd written them over a dozen letters in her head, every night since they'd been gone.

Or maybe it was more like the same letter, over and over.

Dear Mom and Dad,

I'll bet anything you're thinking about us right now. I don't know how this will sound, but I'm not sure if I should think about you two or not. In some ways it feels harder when I do, but I also can't help it.

I've learned some amazing things out here. We all have. And I definitely feel closer to Carter, Vanessa, and Buzz. We've become a real family. But I'm ready to come home, and once I'm there, I'm never going to leave again.

I wish you could see everything we're doing. Actually, I wish you could see a lot of things out here. But most of all, I'm wishing that I'll see you again SOON.

There aren't any stars tonight, so I'll just wish that on my heart.

Love, love, love, Jane

"Ani, what does *issa mekata* mean?" Vanessa asked. Even though she didn't know the answer, some part of her was afraid to find out. This late, quiet moment seemed like a perfect opportunity to learn as much as she could.

"When did you hear that?" Ani asked.

"Chizo said it to Mima," Vanessa answered. "And to Carter, too."

"It is a Nukula phrase that has no true translation," Ani told her. "But it is meant to say, 'You will regret this for the rest of your life.' It is a very serious thing to tell someone."

"Like a curse?" Vanessa asked. The idea of it put a chill through her.

"Not like a curse," Ani said. "More like a prediction, but one that is based on information, not just feeling."

They walked in silence a bit farther, circling the camp. Almost everyone was asleep except for Buzz and a few other runners, sitting near the fire. Mima was snuggled against Jane on the ground, closer than she'd allowed herself to be with them up until now.

"If Chizo becomes chief, can he make life harder for Mima?" Vanessa asked.

"Her life has already been hard," Ani said simply.

"Does she have family?"

He seemed to consider his answer, as always. Even though he'd been helping them since their arrival, Ani was very deliberate with the details he offered.

"She did," he said finally. "Her mother and father were not happy here."

The words landed heavily with Vanessa. "What do you mean? Did they leave her behind?"

"It is not that," Ani said. "They had planned to take Mima away. To leave the island. It is unusual, but it happens."

"And?" Vanessa asked.

"As I've told you, the tides here are very difficult," Ani said.

"I don't understand," Vanessa pushed.

"They did not make it," Ani said.

The message was clear. Mima's parents were no longer alive.

"What happened to Mima?" Vanessa asked.

"She was young but strong. She made it back to the beach alone, and it was quickly known what had happened. To the Nukula, it is very shameful for anyone to wish to leave."

His words turned over in Vanessa's mind.

"So that's why Mima is alone."

"Yes," Ani said. "As a child, you are only as worthy as your family name. Her name has been disgraced, so she has no value. You have experienced her kindness, but the Nukula view her as a pariah."

"So, why even bother trying for a *seccu*?" Vanessa asked.

"If she proves herself in *Raku Nau*, she becomes her own person. She will be treated as an adult, and her life would be much improved," Ani answered, looking over to where Mima slept. "It would mean a new start for her," he said.

"But what about—" Vanessa began, before Ani cut her off.

"I have said more than I should," he told her. "Take your brother and lie down with the others. You will need your rest. Tonight, more than any other."

Vanessa looked at Ani in the dim light from the fire. His face was always so hard to read. But something told Vanessa that he'd just given her exactly as much information as he'd intended. No more, no less. She knew better than to keep asking questions.

"Good night then," she said.

"Good night. Get some sleep," he told her.

"I'll try," she said. But with everything behind them, and everything still to come, it was hard to imagine getting any sleep that night at all.

CHAPTER 14

A long howling call woke Carter. It was a horn of some kind—the blast of a conch shell, he realized.

Someone was shaking him awake. It wasn't just the sound in the distance that had roused him. Buzz was there, yanking him by the shoulder to sit up.

"What's going on?" he blurted out.

"It's starting," Buzz said. His voice was tense. Other runners were moving quickly around the camp.

"Wha'?" Carter managed, but he jumped up, too. His body was ahead of his brain. Everyone was on the go, headed east again.

The sun was barely up. There had been no starting

ceremony. No nothing. Two days in a row.

"Does this thing just . . . start itself?" he asked.

"Yeah," Vanessa said. "I think that's exactly what it does."

They were running now, too. It was a violent feeling, to be asleep one minute and hurrying away from camp the next. There was no indication of who had moved first, and no sign of Ani or the elders anywhere.

They ran in a clump, toward the sunrise. Mima was at the front, while Carter hung back, just far enough to make sure the others stayed together.

Almost right away, the grassy plain near the camp gave way to more woods. The forest was sparser here than in the jungle, so the running wasn't hard. The difficult part was navigating all the other people. Runners ahead of them cut left and right, darting behind trees then quickly reappearing. It was disorienting as Carter and the others worked to keep up.

Quickly, the ground began a steep upward slope. Now the way ahead was marked by a well-worn path in the dirt. It was probably made over generations by previous *Raku Nau* runners, Carter assumed, but there was no way to know for sure. There was no way to know anything right now.

As they moved higher, the valley behind them began to show through gaps in the trees. It soon became clear that they were farther up the mountain than any of them had realized. All the climbing and descending the day before had left them on deceptively high ground.

For a long time, nobody spoke at all. The group of twenty-three runners moved in a cluster along the wooded trail. Mist began to show in the air around them. Carter felt the temperature drop.

When they came out of the woods again, it was onto flatter ground. Looking ahead and behind, Carter could see the tall spires of Cloud Ridge in both directions. They were the same ones that had looked like the spikes of a crown from far away. Now they were like smokestacks, rising up into the thickest part of the fog.

Several runners sprinted ahead and disappeared. The trail seemed to be leading them toward the next spire, looming directly in front of them, but it was impossible to see farther than twenty or thirty yards through the mist.

Carter could smell the ocean as they ran, too. The eastern shore couldn't be too far off now, he thought. But it also couldn't just be that easy. Something else was waiting for them. Some other obstacle, or challenge. That went without saying.

After several more minutes of silent running, the yellowy light of a fire showed up ahead. Coming closer, Carter could also see the male elder from before. He stood near the wide entrance of a cave, where the white mist gave way to a black nothingness behind him.

Shadow Island, even more than Nowhere Island, seemed to be riddled with passages, caves, and caverns, like an underground network. The question was, Where did this one lead?

Stuck into the ground all around the elder was a grouping of sticks. Each one was bound around the top with vine and matted grasses. They were torches, Carter realized. He didn't count them but suspected there were twenty-three in all, one for each runner left in the competition.

Chizo was among the first to have arrived. He'd gone straight for the torches, but as he began gathering several for himself, the elder spoke sharply to him.

Chizo responded immediately and dropped all but one. Then he placed the head of the one he'd kept into the fire.

Right away, a dozen or more runners were jostling for position, lighting their own torches and heading straight into the cave. It wouldn't be dark back there in a minute, Carter realized. Already, he could see the flames inside as the first runners began crisscrossing the space, searching inside for whatever came next.

As soon as Buzz and the others had fire to take with them, they raced into the cavern. Its wide entrance forked almost immediately, lit by the other competitors' torches as they ran in both directions.

"Mima, which way?" Jane asked.

Buzz turned to see which direction Mima would point. His torch *whoosh*ed through the air as he did, and nearly caught Vanessa's hair.

"Careful!" she said, stepping back and nearly knocking Carter over.

"Watch it!" Carter said.

They were going to have to be more cautious than ever in the tunnels. Buzz held his torch closer now, feeling the heat on his face. It added to the sweat of the run they'd made to get this far. Still, there was no time to lose.

Mima seemed as confused as they were. She held her torch in front of her, looking left, right, and then left again. Shouts from one runner to the other echoed around the cave and filled the air with a disorienting blur of noise.

"It doesn't look like anyone knows which way," Buzz said. "I say we just pick a direction and go."

"Go . . . to what?" Jane asked.

"I have no idea," Buzz said. "But we've got to find out."

He chose for them then, and traveled left.

It was getting easier to make quick decisions as *Raku Nau* went along, mostly because the race demanded it. But that was no guarantee of doing this correctly, Buzz knew. All they could really do was keep going and hope they'd made the right choice.

Jane could feel the tunnel sloping uphill as she went. More than once, the passage forked, or another path crossed in front of them. Sometimes those intersections became apparent only when someone's torch showed itself around a corner or raced by in another direction.

Buzz seemed to have a feeling about what to do in this maze, and they continued to follow him, including Mima. It was clear that she had grown to trust them over the past few days, just as they'd come to trust her. Hopefully it would get them all farther in the end.

The passage narrowed, then opened up wide and closed in again as they went. It was easiest to stick to a single-file line. Jane's arm ached from the heavy torch as she held it at her side, running behind Vanessa at a safe distance.

Soon, they came to another fork. This time, there was some daylight ahead. It showed in both directions, where the tunnels curved out of sight. Both ways seemed like potential exits, and both were empty of other runners.

"Which one do you think?" Vanessa asked.

"It doesn't matter," Carter said. "Just lead, Buzz! Pick a way and go."

Buzz nodded, headed left, and continued without another word. Jane and the others stuck close behind.

The light from up ahead made it easier to see the ground, and they moved faster now. Coming around the next bend, Jane saw a good-sized exit waiting for them. Beyond that, there was nothing more to see but wisps of fog.

Finally, they emerged into the fresh air. Straight ahead, the ground dropped away to a sheer cliff. They were standing on a tiny outcropping of rock no bigger than a closet. And the scene that spread out in front of them was unlike anything Jane had ever seen.

First, there was the summit of Cloud Ridge itself. It was a massive wall of earth stretching as far from side to side as it did up and down. But to reach it, they would have to cross the gorge in front of them.

And that was the strangest part of all. There,

in the gray mist, was an incredible bit of Nukula construction, bridging the gap. Jane could scarcely take it all in.

Stretching all the way across the gorge were three levels of intertwining mesh net, bamboo poles, plank bridges, suspended platforms, and roughly constructed ladders—all lashed and secured to the mountain itself. It looked as though it had been there for years. Every element seemed to be attached to at least one other, like a giant interlocking puzzle.

The overall course sloped in an uphill direction, from the ledge where they stood to the far side. And there, standing alone, was Ani. He watched the proceedings with no expression that Jane could make out from this distance. But he nodded when her eyes met his across the space, as if to say, *You made the journey this far. Good.*

Behind Ani, a vine had been strung between two trees. Jane could see a row of sixteen *seccu* hanging there. She'd seen the *seccu* before, around the necks of several elders in the village, along with the two who had been officiating from the start of *Raku Nau*.

Beyond all that, the only thing Jane could see was more mist. It looked as though the crest behind Ani dropped off sharply again, toward the east. Which was where they had to go.

This was it—the end of *Raku Nau*.

Twenty-three competitors were left.

Sixteen *seccu* waited to be claimed.

And one enormous obstacle still stood in the way.

Vanessa's mouth dropped open, but there were no words. The place they'd come to was an enormous natural arena. Behind them, one of the green spires of Cloud Ridge stretched up into the mist, while a backdrop of swirling white behind Ani and off to either side seemed to enclose the whole area within a barricade of clouds.

At Vanessa's feet, the gorge wall dropped straight down. Off to her right, more cavern openings and tiny outcroppings showed in a line. She counted six of them in all. Each one presented a different starting point for the obstacle course. From the spot where they now stood, the way on was a tiny plank bridge. The near end of it rested on the ground at her feet. The far end was lashed to a small platform, maybe two yards away.

After that, they would have to choose whether to continue forward, left, right, or even down. The course had been constructed on three levels. The top two levels consisted of obstacles, all hanging above a vast net fifty feet or more below. The net was made from the same woven mesh Chizo had used to capture them earlier. That meant if someone fell, it would be strong enough to catch them, but there would be no way back onto the course from that far down. The drop was too far and the gorge walls were too sheer.

At the same time, Vanessa realized, there was nothing she could assume about any of this. The wood and bamboo elements were all faded and weatherworn. There was no knowing how long ago this whole thing had been constructed, or how strong any single element was.

"No mistakes now, you guys," she said. "We have to be extra careful."

"No kidding," Carter said, looking down.

More than half of the runners were already out on the obstacles. Others, she could hear, were shouting and echoing around inside the cavern, trying to find a way out.

"Mima?" Vanessa asked. *"Ekka-ka?"* She pointed onto the bridge.

"Ah-ka-ah," Mima answered, though she seemed to be guessing as much as the rest of them.

Even so, Mima planted her torch in the ground, then stepped into the lead position. She put a foot onto the bridge to test it. Once she'd satisfied herself, she quickly ran across, followed by Buzz and Jane.

Then, as Jane reached the halfway point, a sharp cracking sound confirmed Vanessa's fear. The bridge wasn't strong enough.

"Jane, come back!" she said. She and Carter both dropped to the ground, reaching for the end of the little bridge as it pulled away. Both of them got there a fraction of a second too late.

Jane fell to her stomach on the plank as the whole thing flipped into a vertical position, still lashed to the little platform on the other side. Mima and Buzz clung to the platform as it swayed on its one supporting bamboo pole.

"Jane!" Carter yelled. She was clinging to the board with her arms and legs, one foot trying to hook a vine that hung off Mima and Buzz's platform. The vine extended safely to the middle level below, if she could get to it.

"This isn't going to hold for long!" Buzz said. Already, the bamboo beneath the platform was making its own cracking noises.

"What do we do now?" Vanessa asked Carter.

"I don't know!" he said. Both of them stayed on the ledge, reaching for the others, but it was an impossible distance.

"I've got it!" Jane said. She'd just managed to hook the vine with her foot, and she pulled it in close enough to grab—first with one hand and then with the other.

"What are you doing?" Buzz shouted as she slid down the vine rope, headed for a bamboo lattice that waited below. "You're going the wrong direction!"

"It's my only choice!" Jane said. "I'll look for a way back up. Keep going!"

Vanessa watched Jane slide down the twelve-foot vine to reach the next level. Mima had run across a wooden beam from the first platform to another one several feet farther on. Buzz had moved to the right, working his way along side-by-side lengths of bamboo.

It was too late to think about moving through this together. With the little bridge already gone, Vanessa and Carter were going to have to find another way onto the course. And the only way to do that was to head back into the caves.

"Carter, we have to get to one of those other entrances," she said. "Right away!"

"What happened to sticking together?" he asked.

"We don't have that choice anymore," Vanessa said. "Come on! And bring your torch!"

CHAPTER 15

Carter picked up his still-burning torch from where he'd planted it in the ground and slipped past Vanessa to lead the way. He was too amped to follow right now, and it was torture turning his back on Jane, Buzz, and Mima, who were still on the course.

He raced back into the tunnel as two more runners came toward them, the flames of their own torches swaying dangerously small. With the shouting, the open fire, and the close quarters, it was just as chaotic inside the cavern as it was outside. There was no knowing if this challenge was going to go on for minutes or hours, either. All Carter knew was that they had to keep moving.

"This way?" Vanessa asked, pointing right at another fork. This was one they hadn't come to before, Carter thought—but then he wondered if that was actually true. Every twist and turn looked alike in the torchlight.

"Let's try it," he said, but they barely made it another ten steps before a rocky dead end rose up in front of them.

"Other way!" Vanessa said, even as they were turning around.

They doubled back and took the opposite side of the unfamiliar fork. From there, another wash of daylight showed around an upcoming bend. Soon they were outside again, facing the course from another tiny outcropping of rock.

Carter looked down and spotted Jane right away. She was on her stomach, crossing a stretch of vine mesh toward the next small platform. From there, she'd have two options—straight up, if she could climb the bamboo pole that rose from that spot, or forward again, across a plank that would take her toward the center of the course. It was impossible to say which was the better move. The whole arena was crowded with so many possible paths, Carter had trouble even focusing his eyes.

"Jane! Are you okay?" Vanessa shouted down.

Jane paused and looked around. It took her several seconds to spot them.

"I'm gonna keep going!" she said.

"Try to get back up to this level!" Carter shouted.

"Buzz!" Vanessa yelled at the same time. "Do you see a way across?"

He'd stopped on another of the small platforms and seemed frozen in place. The only thing he moved was his head as he looked left, right, and down. Carter couldn't tell if he was terrified or studying the other runners' movements. Maybe both.

From the outcropping where Carter stood with Vanessa, their only way onto the course was a vine-rope swing. That meant jumping, one at a time, grabbing the vine that hung three or four feet away, and using it to propel themselves onto a waiting platform. It was the kind of move that would seem simple in a gym somewhere, or on a playground.

But here, a miss would mean falling two levels down to the mesh that underlay the entire course—and falling out of the competition, too.

When Carter looked down again, he saw one boy had already met that fate. He was at the bottom level, struggling just to get his footing on the net where he'd landed. The look of defeat on the boy's face said everything. There was no way back up.

Carter's mind raced. With one runner out, that left twenty-two runners on the course. And sixteen *seccu* still waiting to be claimed.

Vanessa was weighing their options when Carter made another fast decision.

"Let's go for it," he said, and jumped to the hanging vine in front of them.

Vanessa's breath rushed out of her. There wasn't even time to shout Carter's name. He leaped, grasped the vine, swung forward, and dropped lightly onto the platform a few feet farther away.

It was an impressive move. Even in the rush of the moment, Vanessa was grateful for his skill. And it made her want to do just as well.

Before she even tried, she took another look around. The first runner of the competition was already finishing the course. He scrambled off a final stretch of netting that hung from the gorge's edge and rolled onto the flat ground at the top of Cloud Ridge. Without pause, the boy sprinted past Ani and straight for the line of *seccu*. He reached up as he jumped, snatched one of the necklaces without touching down, and disappeared over the crest.

"Come on, Nessa," Carter said. "We have to keep moving."

"You're right," she said, turning her attention back to him. "Something tells me this is going to be over soon." Already, two more runners were nearing the top. It wouldn't be long now before they'd grabbed their own *seccu*.

Which would mean there were thirteen *seccu* left.

Vanessa eyed the vine rope. Then she jumped.

Her hands closed around the woody texture of the vine. Her body swung forward. She reached with her toes first, arched her back, and let go, flying the last few feet onto the platform. Carter was right there to pull her in as she landed. The platform swayed back and forth. It was solidly built but not well anchored. It felt like landing on the deck of a rocking boat.

As soon as Vanessa could, she looked around, gauging Buzz's, Jane's, and Mima's progress.

Jane was working her way laterally and seemed to be heading for a bamboo ladder on the far side of the next platform—one that would bring her back up to the top level.

Mima was just stepping onto a wooden beam that swung between two vine ropes. As Vanessa watched, the whole thing gave way, just like the small bridge before it, and Mima dropped. She reached for the nearest rope, but it was too late.

"Carter!" Vanessa shouted.

"I see!" he said—but there was nothing they could do.

Mima landed ten feet down, on the next level—lucky enough to crash onto a bamboo lattice like the one Buzz had already crossed. The fall looked painful, but the lattice held.

"Mima! Are you okay?" Vanessa yelled. Mima was still for a moment, but then she sat up, rubbing her arms on both sides. She waved to say she was fine.

It was becoming clear now that not every piece of this course was meant to be crossed. Some elements were solid. Others were like traps. As for how to tell the difference, Vanessa had no idea.

Buzz, meanwhile, hadn't left his spot.

"Buzz, what are you doing?" she called out. "You have to keep moving. Do you want us to come get you?"

"Hang on!" he barked back. His gaze had a familiar intensity to it. He seemed to be thinking something through, but time was not on their side here. When Vanessa glanced to the top ridge, two more *seccu* had been snatched off the line behind Ani. It was down to eleven necklaces.

"Buzz!" she tried again. *"What are you doing?"*

This time, he didn't even respond. His gaze seemed to be following one runner in particular. A Nukula girl. Vanessa watched—glancing back and forth between Buzz and the girl—as the girl scrambled up a vine rope, across one last plank, and over a section of mesh to reach the top of Cloud Ridge, where Ani was waiting.

A moment later, she'd leaped and grabbed a *seccu* on her way out of sight, just like the others before her.

Ten *seccu* left.

When Vanessa looked back again, Buzz was sitting bolt upright on his platform.

"Yes!" he shouted.

"Buzz?" Jane called up from below. "What's going on?"

"Everyone stay where you are!" he said.

"What for?" Carter yelled back.

"I'm going to tell you which way to go!" he said. "Because I just figured this thing out!"

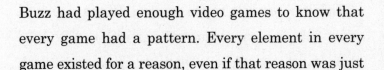

Buzz had played enough video games to know that every game had a pattern. Every element in every game existed for a reason, even if that reason was just to get in the player's way. What if this course was built with the same idea in mind?

So he'd watched carefully. He'd studied the movements of the other runners. And most of all, he'd watched the ones who made the fastest progress. After the first three runners reached the top, Buzz started to see some of the common threads in the paths they were taking.

The obstacles weren't random. There was a strategic design to this thing. A code. And the quicker you figured it out, the faster you got to the top.

The realization was like fireworks going off in his brain, even as the clock kept ticking.

"Buzz, stop messing around!" Jane yelled again. "What are you talking about?"

"I see it!" he shouted. "I know how to do this!"

Like so many patterns he'd found in so many games before, this one went from invisible to obvious as soon as he'd puzzled it out. Now, it was like a line of yellow highlighter marking the way for them.

"Left, left, right, and then right, right, left!" he shouted out. That was the pattern. From each platform, there were directional choices to be made. Some of those choices led to success, some led to dead ends, and some led to a fall. Already, three runners had plunged to the bottom of the course and were out of the running.

The next trick was going to be getting Carter, Jane, Vanessa, and Mima on the right track from their current positions. Only ten *seccu* remained on the vine strung behind Ani. And they'd need to get there in time to secure five.

"Carter, Vanessa! Stay there for now. Jane, you go first!" he yelled.

Already, he'd gauged where Jane had begun the course, and where the left-left-right, right-right-left pattern should have taken her. Except for her last two moves, she seemed to be on track.

It was an amazing feeling of certainty, now that he had it. And the kicker was, nobody but Ani could understand what he was saying. He could shout out all the instructions he wanted to.

First, though, he had to be absolutely sure.

He looked back at the broken bridge where they'd

started. His eyes followed the pattern from there— starting with a left turn off the platform. That was the rope Jane had taken down.

From the bottom of the rope, Buzz's eyes continued to where Jane had taken another left, along the bamboo bridge to the next platform. There, Jane had gone straight instead of right. Which was her first wrong move.

"Jane! Go back to the last platform!" he said, pointing. "Everyone else wait! Mima! Wait!"

He'd caught Mima's attention now, too, but she seemed confused by his instructions. Still, there was only so much Buzz could process at once. He focused on Jane for the time being. She was their best hope at confirming this answer.

"This way?" Jane asked, pointing to the platform she'd left behind.

"*Yes!*" Buzz said. "And hurry!" When he looked across the gorge, two more *seccu* were gone. Eight left. But if this idea was correct, then the rest was going to be easy.

"Now what?" Jane called from the platform.

"Go right!" he said. "Onto that net."

"It doesn't look very strong!" Vanessa shouted from her platform. "Those vines are like strings. Are you sure about this, Buzz?"

"Yeah," he said. "Pretty sure."

"Buzz!" Jane shouted.

"I'm sure!" he called back. "Just do it! Take it all the way to the next platform. Then right again. See that ladder?"

"Got it," Jane said.

Everything seemed to stop moving around him as he watched her execute the next move, also to the right. And sure enough, the net held. After that, the remaining moves went by quickly. Jane took a left turn off the next platform, which brought her up a bamboo ladder, back to the upper level.

"Keep going!" Buzz said. "Left to that platform. Then left again. Then right. It's left, left, right. Then right, right, left!"

Jane was moving even faster now. She'd always been the best climber, and the most agile. It was becoming clear to Buzz—and to Jane, it seemed, from the way she was picking up speed—that he had her heading straight for the top. His mind jumped ahead three more moves, to the patch of ground at the summit of Cloud Ridge, where Ani waited.

"Go, Jane! You've got it! Right, then right, then left again."

It took her down another ladder, across a pair of ropes, back up again, and over a bridge that ended at the far side. Within two minutes, Jane was standing next to Ani, her face beaming.

"Buzz, I can't believe it. You did it!" she screamed.

But there was no time for celebration. Buzz looked back to where Vanessa and Carter were waiting. The good news was that they'd stayed on the first platform near the cave's exit. That meant there would be no backtracking to do.

The problem was with Mima. She'd gone way off course, and there was no language Buzz could use to get her where she needed to go.

"Carter and Vanessa!" he shouted. "Take that balance beam left from your platform, all the way to the next one. Then left again—that means down the pole, and then right off the platform at the bottom. Have you got it?"

"Got it!" Vanessa said, already stepping onto the beam. When it held, she proceeded across with the confidence of the gymnast that she was.

"Mima!" Buzz shouted. She looked up from the ladder she'd been about to climb. *"Fah!* Not that way!" he said, and pointed behind her. She looked back skeptically, but Buzz pointed again.

"Ah-ka-ah! That way!" he said, with as much strength in his voice as he could muster.

She followed his direction, but she still had a lot of careful backtracking to do.

"Okay, Vanessa! Carter!" he said, playing traffic cop now. "You're doing great! When you get there—go right this time. Then right again. Then left. You see it?"

"Slow down," Carter called back. "We're not there yet."

"Well, hurry!"

Finally, he turned and started calculating his own route. His eyes skimmed the nearest elements, checking for his next best move. As he did, his gaze landed on Chizo, staring back at him from below.

Chizo was still on the course—and he did not look happy about it.

CHAPTER 16

Jane threw her arms around Ani. "I can't believe it!" she said. "I made it across!"

"You did well," Ani answered warmly, but without returning the hug. "Now you must keep going."

"What?" she said. She looked back to the course, where Buzz was shouting instructions to Vanessa, Carter, and Mima. "I have to wait for them," she said.

"No," Ani said. "It is time for you to claim the *seccu* that is rightfully yours."

"But, I have to wait—"

"You may not," Ani answered simply. "Each runner must complete the course in his or her own time. This is your time."

He motioned her toward the line of *seccu* that hung just out of reach behind them. Beyond that, Jane saw, was a vast opening in the ground. It was at least fifty feet across, and filled with the mist that seemed to pour over the landscape here.

"What's down there?" she asked. "How can I jump if I can't see?"

"Do you trust that you will be well?" Ani asked.

Jane wanted to say yes, but it wasn't that easy.

"What if I don't do it?" she asked, starting to tremble all over.

Ani waited for a moment, then spoke quietly while barely moving his lips.

"Then I will push you," he said. The words took Jane by surprise. "This is the final test of *Raku Nau*, and there is only one way to succeed," he added. At that, his eyes moved to the opening in the ground, showing her the direction she needed to go.

Jane understood. Once again, Ani was trying to help them in any way he could.

She looked again, over the edge in front of her. All she saw was twenty feet of rock face, and then nothing but boiling fog. It was going to be like jumping into the clouds from above.

Her mind felt split in two. There was nothing about this that felt like a good idea. But there was no choice, either. She had to do it. They all did.

And some part of her wanted—no, *needed*—to do it on her own, without help from Ani.

There was no time to find her courage now. No chance to find another way through this. The sound of other Nukula runners approaching the end of the course pushed her mind to race even faster.

Jane stepped back from the edge several feet. She tried to take a deep breath, but her body was shaking too badly. Ani watched from where he stood, offering nothing more than a steady gaze.

This was all on her now.

She set her eyes on the necklace hanging in front of her, and ran toward it until there was no ground left. Pushing off, she leaped as far as she could. Her hand closed around the *seccu* cord, and it snapped free in her grasp.

Then she dropped.

Buzz's mind surged. So maybe Chizo wasn't great at *everything* in this competition, after all. *Raku Nau* was meant to test competitors in many ways. Ani had told them that, more than once. This course was a whole new kind of challenge—and Chizo wasn't doing well at it. If he made it to the end, he was going to be among the last. It seemed incredible, but the look of angry frustration on Chizo's face said everything.

Still, Buzz had to stay focused. He watched the course carefully, calling out moves to Vanessa and Carter, then figuring his own way to go—left, left, right, then right, right, left.

At the same time, he shouted to Mima, trying to indicate her path with gestures. The course was so multidirectional, it was almost impossible to communicate effectively from this distance.

Soon, Vanessa and Carter had begun using the pattern without any more help from Buzz. They were making fast progress toward the top, and toward the last seven *seccu* that hung there.

Buzz shouted down to Mima once more, pointing her toward the bamboo ladder Jane had used to climb from the middle level to the top. Then he pulled himself across a swinging log to the next platform in front of him.

"We're almost there!" Vanessa shouted back. "Hurry up, Buzz! And Mima! This way!"

"She can't understand you!" Buzz said. "Don't confuse her!"

"I'm not!" Vanessa said. "I'm just trying to—"

"Let me do it!" Buzz yelled, cutting her off. There was no time for discussion. Vanessa and Carter were nearly through, and he was headed toward the last few obstacles he would need to cross before all three of them would be in the same spot—and one move away from finishing. Once they got there, they could go after Mima, or shout and gesture to her the rest of the way.

Buzz stayed low and duck-walked across a narrow bridge, which was really nothing more than half a log suspended between two vines. He ignored the sick feeling in the pit of his stomach and focused on one step at a time. If he fell to the bottom now, it would be nothing more than a completely avoidable disaster.

He reached the next platform as Vanessa and Carter waited on the other side of a bamboo pole that hung between his platform and theirs. It was time to cross right over to them, but the pattern in his head told him otherwise.

"Go that way!" Buzz said, pointing them toward the right. "We're almost there."

"We have to wait for Mima!" Carter said.

Buzz knew Carter was right. They couldn't finish this without her. He looked back, and saw she'd made it back to the upper level again. Now she crouched on a platform, looking left and right.

"Mima!" he shouted. When she looked, he pointed her to the right, sending her across another swinging bridge.

"Listen, you guys," Carter said. "I'm going to go get her."

"No way," Vanessa said. "We're finishing together."

"It's too late for that!" Carter said. "Jane's already

gone. Go find her and make sure she's okay. I'll get Mima. We'll be right there."

Buzz looked at Vanessa, and he could tell she'd already agreed. Sticking together wasn't even an option anymore. And there were only six *seccu* left. Another runner had just pushed past them on the course, run up onto the ridge, and disappeared with one more of the necklaces.

"Buzz!" Mima called out.

He turned to see her waiting. She seemed to understand he knew the way through. Now it was just a matter of getting her there.

"I've got this," Carter said. "I can move through this stuff faster than either of you. Just tell me what she needs to do, and then get out of here! Go find Jane!"

Buzz checked his sense of the route one more time.

"She has to go right off that next bridge," he said. "Then left off the platform. Then it starts over. Left, left, right, then right, right, left—"

"Got it!" Carter shouted after them. "Find Jane! We'll see you down there."

Wherever "there" is, Buzz thought.

"Be quick," he said to Carter,

"You know it," Carter said.

Buzz pulled himself the last few feet, rolled onto the solid ground of the ridge as he'd seen the other runners do, and jumped up. Vanessa came right behind.

Ani was there, watching without a word.

"Thank you, Ani—for everything," Vanessa said.

"Do not stop" was all he said, and Vanessa turned to face Buzz.

"Ready for this?" she asked. Her eyes were wild. She looked as terrified as he felt.

"Not at all," Buzz said.

"Together?" she asked.

"Together," he said.

And with that, they ran straight for the edge at the same time.

Vanessa felt a brief slick of chill air as she passed through the mist. There was a breathless, silent moment of swinging arms when her body tried to curl under her—just before she hit water.

The plunge was freezing cold. She marked her descent, already thinking about how far she'd have to swim back up. Then, as soon as she could, she reversed direction in the water and started kicking.

As she broke the surface, warm air filled her lungs with the first breath. She shook her head, clearing the water from her eyes.

"Buzz?" she shouted. "Buzz!"

"I'm here," he said, not far behind her. When she looked, he was treading in place, and taking in the vast cavern around them.

The bright orange sunlight of a new morning was pouring in, filling the entire chamber with a warm glow. It came through a high, wide opening like a four-story natural arch in the rock walls.

Vanessa looked straight up. It seemed impossible they'd dropped all that distance. The layer of mist that blocked her view of the sky, and the ledge they'd left behind, was like a ceiling of clouds.

For several seconds, it was nothing short of staggeringly beautiful—a stone cathedral under the island. But reality quickly set in. Vanessa knew they had to keep moving. The high walls all around didn't offer any refuge, and Jane was nowhere in sight. It seemed obvious she'd already swum out through the enormous arched opening.

Buzz seemed to have realized it as well. Without any conversation, they began stroking their way through the water and toward the warm light outside. The adrenaline of the jump and the nearing end of *Raku Nau* were enough to keep Vanessa moving. Buzz had no trouble keeping up, either. It was nearly over.

As soon as they'd swum past the mouth of the cavern, Vanessa put her hand on Buzz's shoulder. They came upright again, treading water and looking for the nearest place to stop.

"Over there!" Buzz said, pointing to a stretch of sandy shore off to the left.

This was it. This was the eastern shore they'd been working so hard to reach all this time.

The first details to distinguish themselves were the people. They stood in and among the trees at the upper edge of the beach. It made them harder to see—not just from where Vanessa watched, but also from any potential passing planes or ships.

There were dozens of Nukula, young and old, all gathered there, waiting for the *Raku Nau* finishers. There were several drummers, too, pounding away. A roaring fire was burning in a clearing in the woods, where it looked as though preparations were being made for a huge celebration.

Right now, their next move was clear, but as Vanessa looked toward the horizon, she couldn't help thinking about setting out from this spot. That was what they'd have to do next—somehow—if they ever wanted to find Mom and Dad again.

Finally, there on the beach, somebody came forward. It was Jane. A few of the Nukula tried to stop her, but she pushed through. She came galloping down the sand toward the water's edge, waving them on.

Vanessa smiled through tears as she swam toward her. It was a relief to see that Jane was okay, and to know that they were one step closer to the end of *Raku Nau*. But she also knew she'd feel a lot better after Carter made it down and they were all together again.

CHAPTER 17

Carter knew it was a showdown now.

There were so few left on the course, it was impossible *not* to be aware of Chizo's every move. And once Buzz and Vanessa had disappeared over the edge of Cloud Ridge, followed quickly by two more Nukula runners, only two *seccu* remained.

That was one for Mima, and one for him.

The finish was right there, within reach. Carter was only a few moves away, closer than anyone left on the course. All he'd have to do was cross a narrow bridge of vine mesh, stand up, and claim his *seccu*. But he couldn't yet. Not without Mima.

He turned his focus back to her, repeating the pattern in his mind—*left, left, right, then right, right, left.*

"Mima!" he shouted, and pointed her to the right, across another bridge of two bamboo poles. It looked unsteady, but Mima was strong and agile. She rose on her toes to cross it in three fast strides. Her progress was quick now.

But the same was true for several others. Chizo was coming on strong from the opposite direction. He'd just shinnied up a rope that brought him back to the top level, and put him within striking distance.

From yet another direction, one of the last remaining Nukula runners was closing in on the finish, too.

Carter's mind seethed, weighing the possibilities. There was nothing he could do to slow Chizo, or the other Nukula girl coming on so fast. And Mima was already going as quickly as she could. What they really needed was more time. But that was too much to ask for.

"That way!" he shouted desperately, pointing Mima to another right turn off the platform where she'd just landed. It was one of the rope swings this time. She navigated it with one clean jump.

"And now there!" he said. With a left turn, she scurried on her stomach, across a hanging bundle of bamboo poles.

When Carter looked again, the other Nukula girl had made several more moves of her own. Already, she was launching over the final section of netting that would bring her up onto the ridge.

There was nothing he could do to stop her. The girl sped straight ahead. Without looking back, she landed on solid ground, continued her run, and disappeared over the edge of Cloud Ridge with the second-to-last *seccu* in her hand.

"NO!" Carter yelled. Everything inside of him seized up. It felt as if his heart had just frozen. Now, a single *seccu* hung on the line behind Ani—and that meant something that was impossible to accept. Only one of them was going to reach the eastern shore now.

Mima, Chizo, or me, he thought.

This wasn't how it was supposed to go. He and Mima were supposed to finish together and join the others.

That was the plan. Now it could be only one of them.

And he was the closest of the three.

Carter looked at Mima again. She was less than twenty feet away, navigating on her own. But Chizo was even closer, crossing one last bridge to close the gap between them. The net where Carter waited was narrow. Chizo would have to run right over him to finish first—and he looked prepared to do exactly that.

"Issa mekata!" Chizo shouted, like a war cry, as he came.

Carter hesitated for one more moment—and it was one too many. Chizo was there now. He leaped from the bridge to the net. His feet tangled between Carter's legs as he tried to pass.

And Carter did the only thing it was in his power to do. He grasped the edge of the net with both hands. Then he rolled as hard as he could, flipping the entire thing like a hammock before Chizo could get past.

It wasn't a conscious plan. His gut had always been faster than his mind. Before Carter had thought it through, it was already happening.

Chizo fell first. He lurched sideways, off the net

and into the air. Carter held tight to the vine mesh as he rolled off, too, his legs dangling underneath him. He knew his grip wouldn't last, but he hung on long enough to see Chizo land, two levels down. It was also enough time to see Mima make the last move she needed in order to reach the ridge. Now she was just a few feet away from the final *seccu*.

"Car-tare!" she yelled. She stopped short and turned back toward him.

"GO!" he yelled at her. The vine cut into his fingers. His arms strained, trying to hold on, as the realization of what he'd just done rushed into his mind. Vanessa, Jane, and Buzz were waiting for him. But now it was too late.

Meanwhile, another runner was closing in fast. If he got to the end of the course ahead of Mima, then all this would be for nothing. Still, Mina reached for Carter, losing precious seconds as she did.

"Mima, go!" he yelled again.

There was only one move left, Carter knew. Only one way to make sure Mima made it through. He let go of the net.

She reached for him one more time, but he was already falling—through the air, away from Mima, and out of the competition.

For good.

Jane stood in the shade with Buzz and Vanessa. She stared at the water, trying to see who was swimming toward the beach. They'd been pulled back into the woods by several elders and made to wait there like everyone else.

A figure had just emerged from the cave in the distance, heading for shore as they watched. Jane squeezed Vanessa's hand, barely able to wait another second.

"Can you see who it is?" she asked.

Vanessa shook her head no. "I can't even tell if it's a boy or a girl," she said.

Then a joyous yell came up from a Nukula man and woman in the crowd. It was a clear sign that they'd just recognized their own child in the water. Someone besides Carter and Mima had made it through.

A minute later, a young Nukula girl reached the beach and ran toward her parents with a big smile on her face and a *seccu* around her neck.

"How many is that?" Jane asked. The panic was rising now. She'd been trying to keep track, but with the confusion of all the arrivals, it was impossible to know for sure if her count was correct.

Vanessa and Buzz stood there, still not answering. But the silence spoke for itself.

Then Buzz looked at her. "There were only two left after we jumped," he said.

"That means . . ." Jane said, but she couldn't finish the thought. Not out loud.

"Yeah," Buzz said, his voice thick with emotion. It was all moving so fast, but it was also clear by now. There was only one *seccu* remaining.

Jane wasn't sure what to think, or even what to feel. She couldn't possibly hope for Mima to fail at *Raku Nau*. But just as much, she couldn't imagine coming all this way only to lose their chance of getting off the island. Or getting home. Or seeing Mom and Dad, ever again.

Now it was just a matter of waiting to see who showed up next. Would it be Mima? Carter? Maybe even Chizo?

It didn't take long to get an answer. As Jane stood there, pressed in close between her brother and sister, one last swimmer appeared at the mouth of the cavern, heading toward them with a strong steady stroke.

Jane squinted, desperate to see. She held her breath. And then—

"It's not him," Vanessa said.

There was no emotion in her voice. She sounded numb. It was the same way Jane felt as the words registered in her mind.

She could see the swimmer now, too. It was Mima coming toward them. Not Carter. The sixteenth runner had just reached the eastern shore, and the competition was over.

Whatever they had hoped might happen here was clearly not going to happen anymore. There was no trying to leave Shadow Island without Carter. And, equally troubling, there was no knowing what would happen to him now—or to any of them.

"Vanessa?" Jane said, looking at her older sister's ashen face. Buzz dropped to his knees.

A blast of conch shells and a burst of drumming rose and grew louder around them, along with the whoops and cheers of the Nukula, as the celebration marking the end of *Raku Nau* began.

The story continues in

STRANDED

SHADOW ISLAND

BOOK 3: DESPERATE MEASURES

READ HOW THE ADVENTURE BEGAN IN

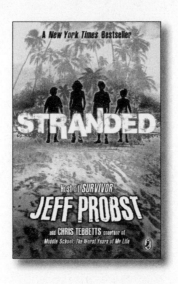

It was supposed to be a vacation—and a chance to get to know one another better. But when a massive storm sets in without warning, four kids are shipwrecked alone on a rocky jungle island in the middle of the South Pacific. No adults. No instructions. Nobody to rely on but themselves. Can they make it home alive?

A week ago, the biggest challenge Vanessa, Buzz, Carter, and Jane had was learning to live as a new blended family. Now the four siblings must find a way to work together if they're going to make it off the island. But first they've got to learn to survive one another.

CHAPTER 1

It was day four at sea, and as far as eleven-year-old Carter Benson was concerned, life didn't get any better than this.

From where he hung, suspended fifty feet over the deck of the *Lucky Star*, all he could see was a planet's worth of blue water. The boat's huge white mainsail ballooned in front of him, filled with a stiff southerly wind that sent them scudding through the South Pacific faster than they'd sailed all week.

This was the best part of the best thing Carter had ever done, no question. It was like sailing and flying at the same time. The harness around his middle held him in place while his arms and legs hung free. The air itself seemed to carry him along, at speed with the boat.

"How you doin' up there, Carter?" Uncle Dexter shouted from the cockpit.

Carter flashed a thumbs-up and pumped his fist. "Faster!" he shouted back. Even with the wind whipping in his ears, Dex's huge belly laugh came back, loud and clear.

Meanwhile, Carter had a job to do. He wound the safety line from his harness in a figure eight around the cleat on the mast to secure himself. Then he reached over and unscrewed the navigation lamp he'd come up here to replace.

As soon as he'd pocketed the old lamp in his rain slicker, he pulled out the new one and fitted it into the fixture, making sure not to let go before he'd tightened it down. Carter had changed plenty of lightbulbs before, but never like this. If anything, it was all too easy and over too fast.

When he was done, he unwound his safety line and gave a hand signal to Dex's first mate, Joe

Kahali, down below. Joe put both hands on the winch at the base of the mast and started cranking Carter back down to the deck.

"Good job, Carter," Joe said, slapping him on the back as he got there. Carter swelled with pride and adrenaline. Normally, replacing the bulb would have been Joe's job, but Dex trusted him to take care of it.

Now Joe jerked a thumb over his shoulder. "Your uncle wants to talk to you," he said.

Carter stepped out of the harness and stowed it in its locker, just like Dex and Joe had trained him to do. Once that was done, he clipped the D-ring on his life jacket to the safety cable that ran the length of the deck and headed toward the back.

It wasn't easy to keep his footing as the *Lucky Star* pitched and rolled over the waves, but even that was part of the fun. If he did fall, the safety cable—also called a jackline—would keep him from going overboard. Everyone was required to stay clipped in when they were on deck, whether they were up there to work . . . or to puke, like Buzz was doing right now.

"Gross! Watch out, Buzz!" Carter said, pushing past him.

"*Uhhhhhnnnnh*" was all Buzz said in return. He was leaning against the rail and looked both green and gray at the same time.

Carter kind of felt sorry for him. They were both eleven years old, but they didn't really have anything else in common. It was like they were having two different vacations out here.

"Gotta keep moving," he said, and continued on toward the back, where Dex was waiting.

"Hey, buddy, it's getting a little choppier than I'd like," Dex said as Carter stepped down into the cockpit. "I need you guys to get below."

"I don't want to go below," Carter said. "Dex, I can help. Let me steer!"

"No way," Dex said. "Not in this wind. You've been great, Carter, but I promised your mom before we set sail—no kids on deck if these swells got over six feet. You see that?" He pointed to the front of the boat, where a cloud of sea spray had just broken over the bow. "*That's* what a six-foot swell looks like. We've got a storm on the way—maybe a big one. It's time for you to take a break."

"Come on, please?" Carter said. "I thought we came out here to sail!"

Dex took him by the shoulders and looked him square in the eye.

"Remember what we talked about before we set out? My boat. My rules. Got it?"

Carter got it, all right. Arguing with Dex was like wrestling a bear. You could try, but you were never going to win.

"Now, grab your brother and get down there," Dex told him.

"Okay, fine," Carter said. "But he's not my brother, by the way. Just because my mom married his dad doesn't mean—"

"Ask me tomorrow if I care," Dexter said, and gave him a friendly but insistent shove. "Now go!"

Benjamin "Buzz" Diaz lifted his head from the rail

and looked out into the distance. All he could see from here was an endless stretch of gray clouds over an endless stretch of choppy waves.

Keeping an eye on the horizon was supposed to help with the seasickness, but so far, all it had done was remind him that he was in the middle of the biggest stretch of nowhere he'd ever seen. His stomach felt like it had been turned upside down and inside out. His legs were like rubber bands, and his head swam with a thick, fuzzy feeling, while the boat rocked and rocked and rocked.

It didn't look like this weather was going to be changing anytime soon, either. At least, not for the better.

Buzz tried to think about something else—anything else—to take his mind off how miserable he felt. He thought about his room back home. He thought about how much he couldn't wait to get there, where he could just close his door and hang out all day if he wanted, playing City of Doom and eating pepperoni pizz—

Wait, Buzz thought. *No. Not that.*

He tried to unthink anything to do with food, but it was too late. Already, he was leaning over the rail again and hurling the last of his breakfast into the ocean.

"Still feeding the fish, huh?" Suddenly, Carter was back. He put a hand on Buzz's arm. "Come on," he said. "Dex told me we have to get below."

Buzz clutched his belly. "Are you kidding?" he said. "Can't it wait?"

"No. Come on."

All week long, Carter had been running around the deck of the *Lucky Star* like he owned it or something. Still, Carter was the least of Buzz's worries right now.

It was only day four at sea, and if things kept going like this, he was going to be lucky to make it to day five.

———

Vanessa Diaz sat at the *Lucky Star*'s navigation station belowdecks and stared at the laptop screen in front of her. She'd only just started to learn about this stuff a few days earlier, but as far as she could tell, all that orange and red on the weather radar was a bad sign. Not to mention the scroll across the bottom of the screen, saying something about "gale-force winds and deteriorating conditions."

The first three days of their trip had been nothing but clear blue skies and warm breezes. Now, nine hundred miles off the coast of Hawaii, all of that had changed. Dexter kept saying they had to adjust their course to outrun the weather, but so far, it seemed like the weather was outrunning them. They'd changed direction at least three times, and things only seemed to be getting worse.

The question was—how *much* worse?

A chill ran down Vanessa's spine as the hatch over the galley stairs opened, and Buzz and Carter came clattering down the steps.

"How are you feeling, Buzzy?" she asked, but he didn't stop to talk. Instead, he went straight for the little bathroom—the "head," Dexter called it—and slammed the door behind him.

Her little brother was getting the worst of these bad seas, by far. Carter, on the other hand, seemed unfazed.

Sometimes Vanessa called them "the twins," as a joke, because they were both eleven but nothing alike. Carter kept his sandy hair cut short and was even kind of muscley for a kid his age. Buzz, on the other hand, had shaggy jet-black curls like their father's and was what adults liked to call husky. The kids at school just called him fat.

Vanessa didn't think her brother was fat—not exactly—but you could definitely tell he spent a lot of time in front of the TV.

"It's starting to rain," Carter said, looking up at the sky.

"Then close the hatch," Vanessa said.

"Don't tell me what to do."

Vanessa rolled her eyes. "Okay, fine. Get wet. See if I care."

He would, too, she thought. He'd just stand there and get rained on, only because she told him not to. Carter was one part bulldog and one part mule.

Jane was there now, too. She'd just come out of the tiny sleeping cabin the two girls shared.

Jane was like the opposite of Carter. She could slip in and out of a room without anyone ever noticing. With Carter, you always knew he was there.

"What are you looking at, Nessa?" Jane asked.

"Nothing." Vanessa flipped the laptop closed. "I was just checking the weather," she said.

There was no reason to scare Jane about all that. She was only nine, and tiny for her age. Vanessa was the oldest, at thirteen, and even though nobody told her to look out for Jane on this trip, she did anyway.

"Dex said there's a storm coming," Carter blurted out. "He said it's going to be major."

"Carter!" Vanessa looked over at him and rolled her eyes in Jane's direction.

But he just shrugged. "What?" he said. "You think she's not going to find out?"

"You don't have to worry about me," Jane said.

She crawled up onto Vanessa's lap and opened the computer to have a look. "Show me."

"See?" Carter said. "I know my sister."

Vanessa took a deep breath. If the idea of this trip was to make them one big happy family, it wasn't exactly working.

Technically, the whole sailing adventure was a wedding gift from her new uncle, Dexter. It had been two months since Vanessa and Buzz's father had married Carter and Jane's mother, but they'd waited until the end of the school year to take a honeymoon. Now, while their parents were hiking Volcanoes National Park and enjoying the beaches on Hawaii's Big Island, the four kids were spending the week at sea and supposedly getting to know one another better.

So far, the sailing had been amazing, but the sister-brother bonding thing? Not so much, Vanessa thought. The weather wasn't helping, either. It looked like they were going to be cooped up together for the rest of the day.

"Is that the storm?" Jane said. She pointed at the large red mass on the laptop screen.

"That's it," Vanessa answered. On the computer, it seemed as if the oncoming front had gotten even bigger in the last few minutes. She started braiding Jane's long blond hair to distract her.

"It's just rain, right?" Jane said. "If this was something really bad, we'd already know about it. Wouldn't we, Nessa?"

Vanessa tried to smile. "Sure," she said. But the truth was, she had no idea how bad it was going to get.

None of them did.

THE ADVENTURE CONTINUES IN

They thought it couldn't get any worse. They were wrong. Being shipwrecked on a jungle island was bad enough. But now that Carter, Vanessa, Buzz, and Jane have lost their boat to another storm, it's like starting over. Survival is no individual sport in a place like this, but there's only one way to learn that. The hard way.

LOOK FOR BOOK THREE!

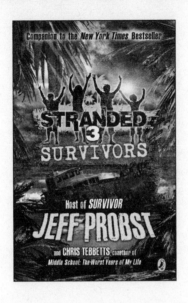

It's been days since Buzz, Vanessa, Carter, and Jane were stranded in the middle of the South Pacific. No adults. No supplies. Nothing but themselves and the jungle. And they've lost their only shelter, and quite possibly their one chance at being rescued. Now they must delve even deeper into Nowhere Island for food and supplies. But the island has a few secrets of its own to tell. . . . With danger at every turn, this blended family has to learn how to trust one another if they stand any chance of survival.

IT HAPPENED ONCE.
IT COULD NEVER HAPPEN AGAIN, RIGHT?

Two months ago, Vanessa and Buzz's dad married Jane and Carter's mom and they became a family. But their adventure really started just two weeks ago when the four siblings were shipwrecked and stranded on a deserted tropical island for thirteen days. Alone. They thought it was over, but now they find themselves on a whole new island, and this time they're not alone. Getting here was a nightmare. Leaving just might be impossible. Because this time it's forbidden.